A NOTE FROM THE AUTHOR

Zach's needed a happy ending from the moment he stepped on the page several books ago. He's one of those characters who has good humor and a lot going on under the surface. In other words, I adored him from the word "go." And I know my readers have, too. So for all of you who have been rooting for Zach and his happily ever after, here it is with the woman he was waiting for, but Ginger was unable to find.

I hope you enjoy this feel-good story about true love, and that you have enjoyed the Veils and Vows stories as much as I have enjoyed writing them.

Happy reading,
Jean Oram
Alberta, Canada 2018

MAIL ORDER SOULMATE

A MARRIAGE OF CONVENIENCE WITH BABY ROMANCE

JEAN ORAM

Mail Order Soulmate: A Marriage of Convenience with Baby Romance
(Veils and Vows book 6)
By Jean Oram

© 2018 Jean Oram
All rights reserved
Large Print First Edition

Printed in the United States of America unless otherwise stated on the last page of this book. Published by Oram Productions Alberta, Canada.

COMPLETE LIBRARY OF CONGRESS CATALOGING-IN-PUBLICATION DATA AVAILABLE ONLINE

Oram, Jean.

Mail Order Soulmate / Jean Oram.—1st. ed.

Large Print ISBN: 978-1-989359-66-2, 978-1-989359-67-9

Paperback ISBN: 978-1-928198-85-7, 978-1-928198-46-8

Ebook ISBN: 978-1-928198-48-2

First Oram Productions Edition: November 2021

Cover design by Jean Oram

ACKNOWLEDGMENTS

A big thank you goes to my Beta Sisters who made sure things were flying straight with the story. In the past we've had some good conversations about things such as which car a hero should drive. This time though we flew through this story as I paused in the middle of its final draft to fly to a conference. (Bad timing!) But as always my Beta Sisters were wonderfully accommodating ladies who I will alway adore. Thank you to Donna Wolz, Margaret Cambridge, Sharon Sanders, Sarah Albertson, J. C., Connie Williams Mechling, Lucy Jones and Erika Howder.

As well, thank you to Margaret C. for your wonderful edits (sorry about the computer and file issues!) and to my proofreaders Emily and Erin for putting a squeeze on the book so I could release the book a week earlier than planned. I suppose folks who aren't Canadian know that American Thanksgiving isn't on the third Thursday of November, but rather is the second last Thursday of November. This only matters when there are five Thursdays in November and your original release day is on the fourth one and you don't want to release on the holiday. Oops!

And as always, thank you to my readers for loving this world and its characters as much as I have. They feel like home.

For Kenzie who said I needed more British Mafia in my books.

Mail Order Soulmate

Zach Forrester considered his living room. The cheerful floral arrangement was a nice touch of color among the muted tones, as was the new, deep burgundy couch. They both added life to the otherwise dull space, making him less likely to notice the brooding gray November light struggling in through the windows. The special-order headlights for his Land Rover, were nice, too. Although the public-issue vehicle tracker wasn't nearly as good as the one he'd used while in the undercover intelligence business.

He checked his credit card statement on his phone and scrubbed at his short hair. It appeared as though his card had taken another hit, thanks to his online shopping bender the night before last.

This was starting to become a costly habit. One he needed to curb.

Zach tossed his phone onto the couch and massaged his aching temples. A few too many whiskeys and a whole lot of consumerism had happened. He supposed his therapy of choice could be worse. But still, something had to change. And soon.

He was failing to adapt to civilian life, failing to pretend he hadn't seen the things he'd seen, hadn't done the things he'd done to keep the country, and sometimes the entire world, safe. Real life was happening around him, but he felt as if he'd been set apart, struggling to act as though he was just like everyone else, that being an agent for almost a decade hadn't changed him in ways that left him altered, unreachable.

Now that he was retired, his new mission was to forget it all, blend in, marry and live a life with a woman who would be okay not knowing every gory detail about the things he'd done in his former career.

However, even the local matchmaker, Ginger McGinty, who never struck out, couldn't find someone for him.

But her husband, Zach's buddy and former partner, Logan Stone, had made the leap from secret life to real life. While he'd seemed surprised when Zach announced he was leaving the service,

Logan had quickly followed suit, the two of them opening a security business that served civilians.

Normal life suited Logan. His reentry had been smooth and effortless.

Zach's reentry, on the other hand, looked more like a shopaholic had gotten hold of Daddy's credit card. Moving himself from South Carolina to the small mountain town of Blueberry Springs a few months back hadn't magically cured him, either.

Zach moved some shipping boxes aside, relieved that he hadn't gone too overboard with this latest spree. He'd needed the couch, and the flowers were cheery. He could manage this. He was still buying stuff he could use. He wasn't blowing it all on trash that would sit in a closet or end up in a landfill.

The doorbell rang and Zach grumbled to himself. How much more from the online world of easy shopping had he decided to overnight ship to himself? There'd been a lull in both the afternoon deliveries and the complaints from his neighbor, George, who claimed the delivery traffic stressed out his dog, Queenie. Zach had assumed that the flowers were the last of the day's shipments, with maybe a few more items coming tomorrow, since in reality, overnight shipping to a small town typically meant one-to-four business days.

He briefly considered doing some forensic

tracking of his online forays, to unearth the last yet-to-be-filled orders so he could cancel them. Although he had to admit it was cheering to receive surprise packages. It was as though all the birthdays that had gone unacknowledged while he'd been out in the field, deep undercover and without family to pass on their well wishes on his special day, had stockpiled. His birthday hadn't been something noteworthy in a very long time.

Maybe that was what Logan had to save him from blowing through his retirement fund: he had someone to spend the holidays and birthdays with. He had Annabelle, his adopted special-needs adult daughter, who lived a few blocks away, and his wife, Ginger, who he'd married as part of his cover during a mission, but had ultimately fallen for.

Zach opened the front door, the security system chirping due to the doorway breach as frigid mountain air blasted him. He was facing a woman in a thin, faded jacket and a backpack. Not a delivery then. Relief washed over him as he gazed at her. She was tall, nearly his height, her blond hair revealing a hint of darkness at the roots, the wavy curls demonstrating a similar softness to her generous curves. She looked like a woman worth holding, someone a man his size could really put his arms around and enjoy, knowing she was there, a grounding force.

Zach blinked and shook himself.

He was lonely. That was definitely the problem. And shopping wasn't filling that hole.

"Zach Forrester?" she asked. She had a British accent and he worked to place it. It wasn't flat like Yorkshire, and it lacked an upper class polish. It was more similar to the classic accent, as if she'd grown up in one of the older downtown neighborhoods or along the edges of London, sneaking smokes and liquor after school, and kissing boys in out-of-the-way corners. Generally getting into a typical teenaged version of trouble he'd never had the time to participate in while growing up.

"Yes?" he replied.

Beyond her on the sidewalk was an infant tucked under a fluffy blanket in a cheap stroller, a diaper bag on the walkway beside it. No car at the curb in front of his two-story. Was she lost? Looking for donations? In need of a safe place to duck into while she called her family—as a man in an unmarked van was following her, and giving her the creeps?

And there he went again. Worst case scenario. Abductions were rare in real life. This whole living and thinking like a civilian was harder than it looked.

"I'm Catherine Tidsdale," she said.

He made a hum of acknowledgment, curious as

to why she'd said her name as though it was one he should know.

"We met on *Email Brides and Grooms*," she continued. "I'm your wife."

CATHERINE DIDN'T KNOW what she should do. Her new husband, a big bear of a man who held himself with a don't-mess-with-me fierceness, while emitting a contradictory aura of warmth and kindness, was staring at her. Just staring. Not blinking. It was as if a fuse had been blown in his mind, only through his striking sapphire eyes she could witness approximately 573 different thoughts zipping by with each passing second.

She had managed to get here a day or two sooner than she'd promised, and she had assumed that her early arrival would be fine. Now she realized the error of keeping her focus only on getting her son and herself here safely.

She tried to subtly warm her hands by cupping them together. It was cold here in the mountain town of Blueberry Springs. Really frigid. Much colder than London usually got, even with that biting dampness that descended each winter. Here, snow had already fallen, and the sun was covered by low, pressing clouds that she guessed was filled with more of the fluffy stuff.

"You're my wife?" Zach inhaled loudly. Then, as though trying the sentence on for size, he repeated himself more firmly. "You're my wife."

He had a nice voice, Catherine decided. It was low and rich, as if he might sing wonderful love songs and add something to them that even Frank Sinatra hadn't been able to.

"Yes," she said.

"We met online."

"Yes."

He started nodding as though things were coming back to him. "All right." He stepped aside so she could come in.

She didn't move, but instead watched him, checking for signs that this wasn't a safe place. There was a gentle curiosity in the way he looked at her, but he also had faint scars that suggested his past hadn't been filled with cherries and roses. He also had well-defined muscles that hinted at discipline, and a stance that said he was ready to fight at any given moment. And while she knew appearances could provide clues, they often weren't enough on their own to determine who was safe to be around and who wasn't.

But when it came right down to it, it was Zach's

slight awkwardness that gave her hope. Hope that he was the kind of man she was seeking. The kind whose own life had been somewhat like hers—lacking perfection and ease—so he would instinctively know that some doors to the past were best left unopened.

Behind Catherine, Xavier began to fuss. He'd traveled fairly well for a two-month-old. There had been times when they'd been on the move while in disguise, where he hadn't been able to settle, but overall he was happy as long as she was moving. She'd had to ditch strollers in various locations as she tried to create cold trails, in case anyone was following them from the UK, opting to carry Xavier against her under a flowing shirt, as though she were an expectant mother again, or tote him about in a picnic basket like she was Little Red Riding Hood off to visit Grandma. He'd been a trooper, and as a result, they'd made it here. Safely.

Now, though, she ignored her son for a moment, focusing on the man in the soft gray T-shirt that stretched over his biceps, apparently immune to the cold that was knifing its way through her jacket.

"Your baby's wet," he said.

"He's not wet."

"Okay," he said, as though agreeing, "but his diaper is wet."

Zach had a calm certainty she identified as wholly American. The Brits she'd known tended to be overly polite and simply give way with strangers. Well, the general population, not anyone from her family, that was for sure. They were pretty good at making their own rules and finding reasons to take whatever they wanted.

But Zach had that something most men sought. Charisma, but with a cool aloofness. He could firmly disagree with you and you'd still like him afterward, and he was the kind of man you wanted to be near, just to see what he'd say next. She'd bet he was loyal above all else, and despite the undercurrent of fierceness she'd noted, that once you were part of his inner circle he'd protect you to the ends of the earth.

Or maybe she was projecting, since she had married a man she'd never met, and needed to rationalize the decision so she didn't commit herself to the nearest psychiatric facility.

Zach had been studying her while she'd been doing the same with him. Thinking. Deciding. It was comfortable, she realized with a start. This big, handsome man had sized her up, taking her in, and she'd been fine with it. And he'd been cool with her sizing him up as well.

She found herself liking him already.

Zach moved past her, and she froze as Xavier's

fussing kicked up into a proper cry. Catherine rushed to elbow Zach out of the way as he unstrapped her son from the stroller.

"Sorry." Zach stepped aside, his subtle scent one she felt she could inhale all day, unlike the overkill cologne her brothers used to wear. In her mind, the smell of cheap, heavy aftershave was linked to cocky men who thought themselves untouchable. Men, she could tell already, who were nothing like Zach. "I should have asked."

There was that flash of hope flickering inside her again. Hope that he was different. Hope that he was similar enough to her to make things work.

She felt safe, and yet there was nothing to base that on. Nothing at all.

She must be more tired from her travels than she'd realized.

"How did you get here?" Zach asked, as Catherine bounced her son in her arms, trying to quiet him as well as shelter him from the harsh wind. Zach gestured to the empty street with his chin, his thumbs tucked in the pockets of his jeans.

"A cab."

She could see the worry and concern hit him. She hadn't called, and he likely knew just how pricey the lengthy cab ride from the closest airport would be. But struck by a bout of nerves and doubts, she'd wanted that last moment to herself to determine whether she was going to truly move to this town, truly choose a stranger. She'd had the taxi sit at the curb for a good five minutes after arrival while she studied the house and pondered the consequences of what she was about to do. Then she'd come up the walk, prepared to catch Zach Forrester off guard, hopeful she'd see the real man and not a polished, rehearsed version ready to impress.

His eyes narrowed. "Where did you take it from?"

"The airport," she replied crisply.

Xavier was still fussing, and through the blanket he was bundled in, she gave his diaper a gentle squeeze, testing for wetness. It was heavy, which meant Zach had been right. Xavier was wet. The man knew his baby cries.

She plucked the diaper bag off the sidewalk. "Where can I change him?"

As she lifted her head to watch Zach answer she found herself face-to-face with him, as he'd been reaching for the bag, as well.

"Let me," he said gently, carefully.

She didn't release the bag, but instead offered him Xavier. Throughout their travels, her son had always seemed to confirm her gut feelings by crying around people she was unsure about, and cooing for those she felt safe with. "Can you carry him? My arms are tired."

Zach expertly scooped up the infant, supporting Xavier's neck as his entire expression and being softened, his focus on the boy in his arms.

"I should have picked you up from the airport," he said, turning toward the house.

Xavier was dwarfed by the man's size, but had settled instantly, his round eyes fixed on Zach's face.

Despite being wired from the long journey and from several months spent in hiding, Catherine could feel her stress drop a notch, just enough that she no longer felt she was about to crack.

Zach talked softly to Xavier as he climbed the several steps up onto the wide wooden porch of the two-story home. The house was a pale blue, with vines of some sort climbing up a trellis on either side of the door. Inside, the place was simply decorated, but cheery. It certainly couldn't be considered drab, with the surprising burgundy chesterfield with lovely floral throw cushions, plus a bright cut-flower bouquet on the coffee table.

Not what she'd expected, but she liked it.

"And what's your name?" Zach was saying to Xavier, his voice a soft rumble, her son still entranced. It looked as though Zach was passing the baby test, as the boy was cooing.

"It's Xavier," she said.

"I'm Zach," he said to the baby. "Our names are at the end of the alphabet, aren't they?" He was heading upstairs and Catherine's heart beat faster.

"Where are you going?" she asked, fear lacing her words despite her wish to keep it hidden. She'd done fine keeping herself safe after Simon's fatal accident. Fine, that was, until their son had been born, making everything feel like a threat to his life. Since then, she'd felt watched and tracked every moment of the day.

That was when she'd realized that after seven months of doing fine, she could no longer do it on her own. That's when she'd started considering Zach's profile on *Email Brides and Grooms*, his name given to her months before by Leo Barrellies, one of the bartenders at the nightclub where she'd worked back in London.

"I thought you'd want to change him on my bed," Zach said. But he promptly turned and descended again. "Maybe you'd prefer the couch?"

She nodded, grateful for his quick change in plans, for being aware that he'd pushed things too far and fast with her, a stranger. He didn't apologize, though, simply laid the child out on the couch so she could tend to him.

She kept her head down as she changed Xavier, handing the wet diaper to Zach, who appeared at the right moment for the handoff. He disposed of the diaper and returned almost immediately.

With Xavier taken care of, she sat with him in her arms, inhaling the scent of his baby shampoo.

Now what? She was across the ocean from home, sitting in the living room of a stranger. Of her husband.

Meeting Zach's steady gaze, she wondered what exactly had made her feel as though this was the safest alternative for herself and her son. But most of all, why she wasn't doubting her choice.

WHILE CATHERINE NURSED her baby on the couch after the diaper change, Zach slipped out the sliding glass door off the kitchen, stepped silently across the deck and out into the frozen yard. He held his phone to his ear, waiting for his friend to answer.

"Come on, Logan. Pick up, pick up," he muttered under his breath, tugging the zipper of his jacket a bit higher.

"Logan here. What's up?"

"There's a woman at my door saying she's my wife."

There was a telling pause. But what it was supposed to tell him, he wasn't sure. Did his friend think he'd finally cracked? Did he think this was a joke, or was he trying to figure out how Zach had evidently married someone he obviously didn't know and had never met?

How did you marry someone over the internet?

Logan let out a snort of laughter before controlling it and replying soberly, his Australian accent especially thick, "Is she of the blow-up variety?"

"Not funny." Zach's voice was tighter than his late grandmother's embroidery stitches.

"Right. So you had a few too many and married someone off those mail-order-bride sites you keep teasing Ginger about?"

Even after Zach caught the bouquet at a mutual friend's wedding, Ginger still hadn't been able to find him someone, after nearly a year of searching. Now it looked as if all Zach had needed was to go online and click "I do."

"That appears to be the story," he replied, pinching the bridge of his nose. Zach was embarrassed that he'd lost control of himself, impacting the lives of others in the process, and didn't even recall doing so. A good agent didn't do that.

He was no longer an agent.

He supposed that was probably for the best, wasn't it?

"So are you going to keep her?" Logan asked.

"She's got a baby." And she hadn't told him she was coming—or had she? And Zach, having forgotten everything, hadn't logged in to receive her message, and as a result was a no-show, forcing her to take a long and expensive cab ride to Blueberry Springs?

He was a horrible human being.

"So?" Logan replied. "You like kids, don't you? Instant family."

"She looks…scared."

"Try talking to her."

"I have."

"And?"

"She took a cab from the airport with nothing but a stroller, a diaper bag and a backpack." Something wasn't right with the scenario, and it wasn't just that a seemingly sane woman believed it was appropriate in this day and age to marry someone you didn't know. As well as bring your infant son along for the ride.

But that glint of fear that had sliced through Catherine's steady gaze… What was that about? She hid it well, but he was trained to catch things like that. He didn't believe the fear was simply about him or the situation.

It was something else.

"You forgot to pick her up?" Logan asked, disbelief lacing his voice, as well as a measure of disappointment.

"I didn't know she was coming."

Logan's tone turned thoughtful, telling Zach his pal was scooting into brainstorming mode. "Escaping an abusive partner maybe?"

The idea made Zach's insides seize and smoke come out his ears.

"Hiding from the law?" Logan offered. "I can run a background check on her. What did you say her name was?"

"We're not agents anymore." Zach pinched the bridge of his nose again, stomping down a circle of snow with his boots, wishing they could indeed run a check and get the full story on the woman in his living room. "We aren't authorized to dig into people's lives. Especially without a valid reason." He straightened his shoulders, pulling in a lungful of cold air. "And anyway, I'm starting this whole new-leaf thing where I try and act like a civilian and not assume the worst in everyone."

"So she's cute," Logan said.

Zach paused, recalibrating swiftly. Cute? He'd been trying to avoid sizing her up, as she was a single mom and therefore not fair game. She belonged to someone.

Him, apparently.

She wasn't single. And neither was he. Shouldn't he have a document in his inbox saying he was married or something? He was obviously worse off than he'd thought.

But was this woman fair game?

He didn't quite think so.

Logan was waiting for a reply about Catherine's looks.

"Yeah, she's cute," Zach said. "Great curves. Blonde." He could feel some of the tension that had been coiling inside him release a little.

Logan let out a chuckle. "Natural blonde?"

"Nope."

"Your type then?"

Zach didn't reply, but felt the hint of a smile.

"Does it seem like her head's on straight?" Logan asked.

The way she'd slowly sized him up, along with her quick, sweeping glances, told him she wasn't naive or oblivious to the crazy severity of this unorthodox situation. She'd tested him when she'd passed her child off to him, using the infant like radar, a detector that sought out the good and bad in the world.

"She's resourceful," he said, still forming a full judgment of her.

"So she's smart," Logan confirmed.

"Yeah." A smart woman doing something stupid. Definitely a story there.

Then again, flip the mirror on him. He'd married her, hadn't he? Definitely a story here, too. Maybe he shouldn't think about this too long and hard.

"Think she's going to want to know everything about you?" Logan asked quietly.

An agent's worst fear. The request to reveal deeply personal, and sometimes classified, information as a form of intimacy. The one thing none of them could deliver. With that wall between them and their spouses, most agents didn't stay married long. At least not the active ones.

"My gut says she doesn't want to tell me about her life."

"Sounds like a perfect match. The two of you can play don't-ask-don't-tell when it comes to your pasts. I vote you keep her around and see if the relationship pans out."

"I don't know her."

"We all have to start somewhere. Ginger and I started our relationship based on a lie and look where it's taken us."

Good places.

"So...I keep her and see where it goes?" Zach shook his head and frowned. It felt like he was talking about a stray, which in a way, maybe she was. If she was smart, resourceful and willing to marry a stranger, then something was going on in her life. And chances were she needed shelter, protection.

And that was his calling card.

No, no. He was putting too much into it.

He didn't have a calling card any longer, unless it was for installing home security systems that beeped every time the front door opened.

It was possible she'd simply found single motherhood too overwhelming. Her presence didn't have to mean something big and dark. A hundred years ago this kind of marriage situation was commonplace, and arranged marriages tended to do well because there weren't unrealistic romantic expectations.

And that was all kinds of perfect for a man like him.

Although, come to think of it, maybe the two of them weren't true strangers. They must have had conversations online before marrying. All he had to do was find the site, log in and see what they'd chatted about.

Easy. He'd have her story in no time. Including where the baby's father was.

"You want to pop by and give me a read on her?" he found himself asking, his plan of action in place.

"Why don't you call in a favor and run a check on her?" Logan suggested.

"She's my wife."

"And?"

"And I'm trying to do this normal-life stuff. That doesn't include running background checks and getting full dossiers. It means having conversations with people. Plus, I could get the guys in trouble for using agency resources for an unauthorized domestic situation."

"Fair enough, even though it hasn't stopped us in the past."

"We were working with Scott." From time to time the two of them had helped the underfunded, short-staffed local police officer, Scott Malone, with the odd case, which more often than not had led to them calling in favors from old associates. In other words, collecting dossiers on perps so they could lock them up faster.

It was definitely rewarding having friends in high places. But in those cases he'd felt justified in reaching out, and with this he didn't.

"I'm plotting out that security system over at Mandy's new brownie factory in Derbyshire," Logan said, "but I'll come by tomorrow to run the plans by you. Make sure your new wife's home."

"Thanks."

"I've got your back, mate. Treat her like a guest. Make her feel safe."

"Safe." Right. He could do that. He'd spent a career keeping people safe.

"And…"

"What?"

"Just be yourself."

"What's that supposed to mean?"

"You're a babe magnet." Logan paused, his voice lowering. "And remember…"

"Condom? I know. I'm not new to this."

"Dude, she just got here. She has a baby."

"Right." Zach squeezed his eyes shut. Where had that answer come from? He wasn't one to push things or hurry women along. And a woman like Catherine needed space. A lot of it.

Which was good, actually, because even though he'd apparently been looking for a wife online, he wasn't looking for love. He wasn't ready for something like that. Not yet. Maybe not ever.

"But yeah, when the time comes," Logan said, "that's always a good plan. What I was going to say is that you tend to make wise decisions while under the influence of the internet. She might just be the one you've been waiting for."

Zach ended the call, Logan's teasing words about Catherine, a curvy woman with an irresistible British accent, being the one he'd been looking for all his life echoing in his mind.

And to know if that was true, all he likely had to do was slip upstairs to his computer to read their forgotten chat messages before their next conversation. Because, after all, they had been enough to make him decide to marry her.

"*A*re you hungry?"

Catherine looked up to find Zach standing in the doorway, his smooth, deep voice making her senses tingle, his offer of food causing her stomach to rumble. She blinked, processing his question, trying to rein her body into a somewhat neutral zone so in her exhaustion she didn't do something embarrassing. Such as cry. Or ask him how often he worked out to achieve such amazing arms. Arms that looked as though he could sweep her up and carry her through any storm.

She stopped burping Xavier, realizing she'd been absently doing so for several long minutes, trying to sort herself out while Zach had been outside, then upstairs. Xavier hadn't been very hungry, but feeding him had given her a mini-escape from having to talk to Zach, allowing herself to slowly absorb her surroundings. The security system motion sensor in the corner with a built-in camera. The window sensors that would announce a break-in. The baseball bat sitting in the umbrella stand, which was strangely located at a hallway crossroads. Was this sleepy-looking mountain town actually a hotbed of crime? Or was Zach just serious about his security?

Oddly enough, the sophisticated system didn't make her feel watched or uncomfortable, just a little safer in what could be her and Xavier's home.

This was it. She was here. Married.

But now what? This was pretty much where her plan ended.

"Catherine?" Zach said gently.

Right. He'd asked if she was hungry.

"Yes, a bit. Thank you."

"The kitchen is this way." Zach led her through an archway to a small dining area with sliding doors to a patio. To the right was the kitchen, spacious and open with lots of counter space, the kind of setup a mother of five would drool over. There was a large island workspace, a double sink beneath a big window overlooking the backyard, and plenty of cupboards, as well as a pantry that could house enough food to get a small family through an apocalypse.

Not that she was calling them a family. Or anticipating an apocalypse. To get here she'd followed every precaution, and she felt secure knowing her past had been left behind. Her old life was right where it belonged—in her rearview mirror and losing ground with every step forward she took.

"Help yourself to anything," Zach was saying. "The whole house is yours. Well, I have a home office upstairs, but we can turn that into a nursery if you'd like."

She bounced Xavier lightly, smoothing his wispy dark hair, overcome by emotion. Calling a room a nursery made it all feel so real.

"What do you like to eat?" Zach asked, digging through what looked like a well-stocked fridge. He turned to face her and she struggled to appear unaffected. "In our chats you said you like Italian."

She liked a man who remembered details. And according to his reply, he liked Italian, too. As well as playing with technological gadgets. Hence the security system?

"I don't want to be a bother."

He watched her for a second. "I could make spaghetti."

"That's a rather large lunch."

"I'm sure your stomach thinks it's well past suppertime." He was already opening a can of tomatoes, dumping them into a pot that he set over low heat. In the sink he began filling a large pot with water for the noodles. "What time is it in Cyprus?"

She'd spent only four hours in Cyprus—a layover of sorts. But it was the issuing country for her fake passport and she figured it was obscure enough that nobody would ever question her about what it was like to have lived there.

"Don't put yourself out. I'm all right," she said, her stomach grumbling at her and proving her a liar.

Zach moved the water to the stove and turned on the burner. "It's nice to have someone to cook for." He glanced at Xavier, who was dozing in Catherine's arms. "Do you have more stuff coming along?"

"More stuff?" she asked, dreading the question, as well as the cost of outfitting them both with everything they'd need, as they'd left most of their possessions behind.

"A crib? Toys? Clothing? That sort of thing?" He plucked an orange from a small fruit bowl in the middle of the island, set it squarely on a cutting board and started deftly slicing it into thin wedges, like half-moons. Once finished, he slid the board toward her and went back to tending his sauce, as well as the ground beef he had frying.

"Are you a chef?" He had a practiced, efficient way in the kitchen.

"I was a cook for a few months while I was in the army. Maybe we can borrow a few things until your stuff arrives."

"I sold most of it. It was too much to manage…" She trailed off, looking to the side, pretending to be interested in the African violet sitting on the counter. To her surprise, it was real. She shifted Xavier higher on her shoulder so she could rub one of the velvety leaves. "I thought these were fussy and difficult to grow."

"That's what I'm told." He wiped his hands on a towel as the doorbell rang. "Help yourself to water if you're thirsty. Glasses are in the cupboard by the fridge." He gestured vaguely while heading to a narrow hallway that ran alongside the under-the-staircase pantry. She assumed it led around to the entrance so people didn't always have to walk through the archway and living room to reach the rest of the house.

The security system chimed, indicating the front door had been opened.

"I heard you could use this."

Catherine risked peeking around the corner, catching a glimpse of the front entry. Beside Zach was a tall, fit-looking man carrying a frilly white bassinet attached to a matching stand.

Catherine stepped back, the timing of its arrival sending goose bumps down her arms.

"Oh, hello!" The man had spotted her, his face breaking into a large smile. He set the bassinet down and stepped around it. "Welcome to Blueberry Springs."

"Thank you."

He kicked off his snowy boots and, moving toward her, thrust out a hand for her to shake. "I have a friend from Dover. What part of England are you from?"

"I'm Catherine," she said. "I'm from Cyprus."

"Cyprus? That's a trip and a half with a little one. You must have fallen pretty hard for ol' Zach." He grinned at the man, whose cheeks had turned pink. "I thought Ginger was still playing matchmaker. I guess international online dating is the next big thing. And…marriage?"

Catherine nodded. She'd been surprised when the website had emailed her paperwork, saying they could legally wed online. That it was some sort of loophole in international agreements the site had found and could apply to marriages.

"This is Devon Mattson," Zach said, still looking embarrassed. "He's the mayor."

Devon tipped an imaginary hat. "At your service."

Him being mayor didn't explain how he knew about Xavier. Zach could have mentioned she was coming, but she hadn't once mentioned her son while chatting online, as it had been too risky. While she knew that was a massive omission, nobody back home knew about Xavier and she planned to keep it that way. She'd had her fingers crossed that having a baby wouldn't be a deal breaker for Zach, and so far he hadn't said a word, which led her to tentatively assume all was good.

"How did you know I have a baby?" she asked Devon.

He laughed. "Welcome to the town of Blueberry Springs. Nothing stays a secret for long."

Catherine felt the cold hand of dread squeeze her stomach.

"Especially not babies." The mayor headed toward the door. "I'll get out of your hair, as you must be tired from your trip. Just thought you could use a bed for your little one."

"How much do you want for it?" Catherine moved to the frilly bed, mentally assessing its price. She wasn't sure how much it would be worth, with the exchange rate and differences in the value of used goods.

"When he outgrows it, just bring it back," Devon said. "We might be ready to pop out baby number two by that time."

Something for nothing? There had to be a catch. And Catherine hated catches. She wanted to know what was owed before she accepted anything. Even the temporary use of a baby bed.

"I'd be more comfortable giving you something for it," she said.

"Just babysit for us once or something. But seriously, don't worry. It's just sitting around collecting dust. We'd prefer someone gets some use out of it."

Catherine assessed the sincerity in Devon's gaze, forcing herself to relax, to accept the offer. She needed the bed, didn't she? And babysitting was an acceptable exchange if he truly did expect something in return.

"Olivia's expecting?" Zach asked.

Devon grinned like he was the luckiest man on the planet. Zach grinned back and clapped him on the shoulder, offering a hearty "Congratulations." His reaction told Catherine that he didn't mind having babies around. Not at all. And that Xavier would not be a deal breaker.

As she turned back to the kitchen, so her wet eyes and tremendous relief would go unnoticed, she thanked the heavens for the unexpected gift of Zach, a man who continued to knock her slightly off-kilter and seemed almost too good to be true.

ZACH WATCHED Catherine work her way through a heap of spaghetti. With the first bite her lashes had fluttered and a low moan of pleasure had escaped. She was indeed a fan of Italian food, as her profile had said. He had to admit, having a pretty woman moan over the meal he'd whipped up stroked his ego in a way that made him want to try making a lot more Italian dishes, as well as take a more thorough look at their online chats.

"How did Devon know I needed a bassinet?" Catherine asked. She was more than halfway through her plate now, her baby cooing in the bassinet beside the table.

He'd noted how she'd been taken off guard by Devon's timing as well as generosity, causing a sense of caution to roll in. The timing, he had to admit, had been uncanny.

"Welcome to Blueberry Springs," he said wryly, "where everyone knows your business. Sometimes even before you do."

And yet he still knew very little about *her* business. After the quick call with Logan, he'd slipped online while she'd still been feeding Xavier and had found a rather short thread of messages that had gone back and forth between them. It sounded as though they'd mostly used the live texting chat feature, which didn't seem to save messages. In other words, there was little to go on in terms of the history of their wooing, and his memory wasn't bringing up much other than some flirtatious banter, which had been fun.

He still hadn't quite wrapped his mind around the legalities of an online marriage or how he'd managed to forget so much. But she was here and he was in it. There was nothing to do but move forward.

He'd read the first message, where she'd outlined a bit about herself, which was a decent start. She liked Italian food, as well as James Bond movies—so would she like being married to a real-life James Bond if she ever found out about his past? Zach hoped so. She hated bodies of water where you couldn't see the bottom. Despised liars. Wished she knew how to knit. Wanted to belong to a book club. Wished to donate more of her time to local charities. And a few other tidbits that said less about her than he'd like.

Catherine's eyes had darkened slightly as they spoke about Devon and his timing, and her brow had furrowed. Zach could tell she didn't like having people in her business, which was something he understood. She wasn't used to small-town generosity, which was based on the assumption that whatever went around came back again soon enough.

"You're from the city?" Zach asked, idling

twirling noodles around his fork. He'd grown up in Philadelphia, on a street that had mostly kept to itself, other than the lady next door who had more kids than she could handle. With that being his last real neighborhood experience, he'd found moving to Blueberry Springs disconcerting. Given the community's well-meant but snoopy ways, he'd found blending in and disappearing into a crowd nearly impossible. For one thing, there were rarely any crowds. For another, he was the new guy in town and therefore had a certain mystery that drew flocks of curious people, leaving him feeling as though his every move was being watched. Not good for a man who'd spent the past few decades striving to remain invisible, allowing him to go anywhere and overhear everything.

After a few months, because Logan had instructed him to ride it out, he'd discovered that in his new life as a personal security agent—mostly installing puppy cams, a nickname Logan had given home security systems that were more about checking in on the dog while at work than about catching thieves in the act—having a community on the watch was a good thing. Someone always seemed to have heard or seen something and was more than happy to talk about it. Even though it sometimes made Zach feel as though his services were redundant, there were enough cases with challenges to keep things interesting.

"I grew up in the suburbs," Catherine said.

"In Cyprus?"

"No." She met his eye.

He could tell she was being truthful, and yet not helpful. Was she simply reserved? Or was it something else?

"You grew up near London. Southwest, I'd bet? Maybe Egham? Old Windsor?"

Catherine's eyes widened in surprise before narrowing.

"Your accent," he explained. A classic London accent with a working-class roll.

"You're an expert?"

"I had a colleague from there." Mostly true. Although the arms dealer he'd put away certainly wouldn't call him anything as jovial as a colleague. "You say some of your vowels the same way."

She gave a polite smile and picked up her plate, but Zach thrust out his hand, covering her free one. "I get it. You have boundaries and don't want to share your past. I won't pry. But I do need to know a few things."

Catherine's eyes were clamped to his hand, her breathing shallow. He didn't release his gentle grip, and she didn't pull away. There was a warmth from their touch traveling up his arm, almost distracting him from asking what he needed to know.

"Are you wanted by the police?" he asked.

She shook her head.

"Does Xavier's father know you're here?"

Catherine looked up, her eyes sad. "He passed away nine months ago."

Zach's hand slid off hers.

A widow. A single mom.

Tired and alone. That could explain the fear. The mystery in her past she wanted to leave behind.

Was that all it was? He had a feeling there was more, and that she wasn't ready to reveal it to him. But if he went digging like Logan had suggested, then he wasn't giving their relationship a chance, was he? He would know things about her and that would change the situation. It wouldn't allow her to give voice to her personal stories, to trust him with them. He'd know, because he *hadn't* trusted her.

The fact that he was having this conversation with himself told him one thing: despite the shadows in her past, he wanted to give this relationship a real shot. Like a normal man would.

A normal man who'd married someone online.

Okay, so he wasn't a poster boy for "normal" yet. Big deal.

The question was, why was she here? Why had she said I do?

And why had he?

He was running from his own past, but what was Catherine running from? Grief or something else?

Whatever it was, his gut told him that the unpleasantness in her past wasn't imminent. She'd be more on edge, more emotional if it was. That meant he could afford to give her some time to reveal herself to him before he asked the boys back at the agency to run a check on her. He'd try the "real" way first. What was that called again?

Sharing?

He could give it a go.

"What are you hoping for with this relationship?" he asked.

She shifted, no doubt uncomfortable by his directness.

"Sorry for being so blunt, but if we share our expectations I think it'll help."

She nodded slowly.

"Do you need someone to pay the bills while you stay home with Xavier?" he pressed. "Do you need a partner? A friend? A father for your son? A true spouse and more kids?" The idea of that last one made his chest hurt. What would he say if that was what she was hoping for?

He wanted that. Of course he did. But he wasn't so certain he was capable.

For a moment he thought she was going to excuse herself and avoid the question. Instead, she tipped her head thoughtfully, her focus hazy as she said honestly, "I'm hoping for a fresh start. A quiet town that's perfect for raising kids. A man who'll be at my side. Just someone who…" She briefly met his gaze, a vulnerability exposed for a brief moment. "I want quiet. A life with football—that's called soccer here, isn't it?—and a minivan and knitted woolly jumpers. Someone to sip tea with me on the patio and watch the sun set." Her lips twisted slightly and she shook her head. "That's a tall order."

"It sounds normal to me."

"I'd be happy having a partnership that values caring and kindness. One that offers support as well as independence."

Well, he'd guess that her deceased beau hadn't been awesome in the family department. Not that he'd had much of a chance, seeing as she'd likely been about two months along before he was permanently removed from the family photo.

Catherine's blue eyes were focused on him again. She blushed, as though realizing she'd revealed more than she'd intended. And yet she held his gaze, silently asking if he could provide any of those things.

Zach drew a deep breath, his chest tight as he envisioned the life she'd outlined. He wanted that, too. It wasn't the moon, just a reasonable slice of contentment.

"I'm sorry," she said quickly, her cheeks pinking even more. "I'm overtired. I get sentimental sometimes."

She stood, and Zach swallowed over the lump in his throat. "That all sounds pretty good to me. Maybe we should take baby steps." What did people do when they first started dating? "Like start with coffee?"

She let out a shaky laugh and he loved her for not being offended, for seeing the humor in their situation.

He stood as well, helping her clear the table. "So you're not looking for love?" He was embarrassed by the way his words came out, awkward and husky.

She gave a quick shake of her head.

Of course she wasn't.

He was a fool to have asked. The father of her child had passed away less than a year ago. She was grieving. People didn't mail-order a spouse because they hoped for a soulmate. They just wanted somewhere to belong, to fit, so they were no longer alone.

"Are *you*?" she asked. Her eyes were dark and wide as she awaited his answer.

He gave a light huff and pushed a hand through his hair. "Don't know that love is in the cards for me."

"Bad relationships?" she said carefully, as though unsure how much they could ask each other.

"Nah, just never really happened for me." He stacked the dishes on the counter over the dishwasher and began running water for the pots. "How about you?"

"Maybe." She gave a quick shrug that told him she had found love but was still feeling its sting.

"You don't know?" he asked, aware he was being a bit cheeky. But he was curious. Curious how life had treated—and obviously managed to beat up—a beautiful, strong woman like Catherine.

"I thought maybe I had..." Her gaze had softened, focused on the distance as though watching a memory float past. "It doesn't matter." She opened the dishwasher and began setting plates and cutlery neatly inside, maximizing space, her system eerily similar to his. "Neither of us is looking for love, right?"

"Right." He began washing the pots, then

stacking them in the drainer so they could air dry. "We're looking for companionship." He glanced her way.

Catherine avoided meeting his eyes and finished with the dishwasher, then took the tea towel off the oven door handle.

"If you're tired you don't have to help."

"It's nice to do something homelike and grounding after—" She cut herself short.

"After?"

"It feels like I've been traveling a long time," she said quickly, her moves suddenly jerky. "Xavier had colic for the first two months and I developed some bad meal habits. Just…surviving, right?"

"I can imagine."

They worked together in silence and Zach wondered just exactly what her living conditions had been like in Cyprus with a colicky baby. Judging from her body language it hadn't been good.

"Were your parents divorced?" he asked, curious if there was more to her not-looking-for-love story than simply being a grieving mother in need of help. In other words, how soon would she leave him once she was back on her feet?

Why was he even thinking that way?

Because he'd been trained to prepare for the end of a mission as well as the operation itself.

This isn't a mission, he reminded himself. *It's life.*

"No," she said. "They stuck it out. Yours?" By her tone he gathered that her parents had fought a fair amount and hadn't had a magical marriage.

"They didn't officially divorce and I suppose they're still out there somewhere." Assuming they haven't overdosed on drugs. "I was raised by my grandmother."

"Is she still with us?"

He shook his head, noting how she'd carefully avoiding asking about his parents. His grandmother had been his whole world, his family. Once she was gone he'd been adrift, taking increasingly dangerous missions as he worked his way up the ranks in the military, then increasing the number of secret missions he accepted until he found himself deep in the intelligence business. His grandmother had taught him many skills that still served him well, and they had helped him through difficult times. Patience, kindness, understanding, how to cook, how to laugh.

But not how to get over her loss.

Catherine and Zach had finished the few dishes and stood staring at each other for a long moment. Her gentle gaze was taking him in, trying to see more than he was willing to reveal.

She placed a hand over his. "I'm sorry."

He jerked in surprise at the depth of her sincerity, at how much she must have seen. Or maybe he was just used to army men grunting their apologies when they came across that personal history tidbit before moving on.

He turned away. "She's been gone some time now."

"You're alone though, aren't you?"

He gave a minute nod, his back muscles tightening. "Are you?"

As he wiped down the cooled stove, he could hear her behind him as she let out a long, slow breath before saying, "By choice."

He tossed the cloth in the sink, and she gave him a quick smile that looked as though it hurt her cheeks.

He didn't have to ask if she wanted to talk about it to know the answer was no. Some parts of a person's past weren't fair game when it came to idle get-to-know-you conversations. In fact, they might never be.

Catherine woke with a start, uncertain where she was. She hadn't slept so soundly in months. Possibly even a year.

Swinging her legs over the side of the bed, she rubbed the sleep from her eyes as the past year came back to her. Her father and the rest of the Davies gang, informally known as the British Mafia, had been arrested during a sting operation just days before her boyfriend's death. Simon had been one of the nightclub's managers, and she hadn't yet figured out how to tell him she was pregnant when a car accident had taken his life.

Just about every Davies family member, and everyone close to them, had been brought in on charges during the sting operation. Including Simon and herself.

She'd left home at age sixteen, wanting nothing to do with the lying, cheating and scheming that went on around her. She'd returned only to attend her mother's funeral a few years ago, and had naively believed she'd separated her life from her family. But little had she realized that the nightclub where she'd been working as an events coordinator for the past seven years, booking headliners and constantly making it the place to be in London, had actually been a front for her father's gang. The worst part was that Simon, manager of the club, may have been involved in the backroom money laundering scheme, and she'd made it easy by constantly making their profits hit the roof each and every month.

When the officers put the pieces together for her, building a picture of her naivety and betrayal, she'd vomited all over the interrogation room. She'd been released fairly quickly after that, with no pending charges.

Simon had been released hours later, and when he'd died in a suspicious accident days later, it had sealed things for her. Her child was not going to grow up anywhere near her father, brothers, cousins and their associates. They already assumed she was a snitch who'd cut a deal, allowing her to walk away without charges while they'd been put behind bars. That put a target on her back.

And Simon…she still wasn't sure whether simply being associated with her had led to his "accident" or if he'd been playing both sides and had paid the price. Either way, the man she'd been involved with was dead, and she feared it wouldn't be long until she joined him, or her child grew up to face a seemingly good offer—like she had with the club's primo events coordinator job—that was simply too good to refuse.

She was breaking the cycle. Saying goodbye to the fear and incessant crime. She was moving beyond the reach of her family's control once and for all.

By the time a frantic Leo, her bartender friend, had caught up with her the day before Simon's funeral, she'd already prepared herself to go into hiding. He'd helped, explaining how and where to get a fake identity, then shoved several *Email Brides and Grooms* profiles into her hand, including Zach's, saying that might be a good way to lie low.

She'd scoffed at the idea of marrying herself off, but had agreed that disappearing would be wise. So instead of going husband shopping, she'd taken the cash she'd kept hidden at home and had gone underground, using a variety of fake names and working small jobs under the table in various countries, until Xavier was born in Honduras.

Her family had looked for her after she'd fled, and stories of her disappearance had surfaced in the news. But after their surprisingly quick convictions six months after their arrests—a mere three months ago—they'd grown quiet, apparently no longer in need of her as an ally, or else the reporters had lost interest in the missing woman and the lack of leads.

She'd continued to lie low up until Xavier's birth, staying on the move and hoping she was safe. But Xavier had been a colicky baby and by the end of the past two interminable months compounded by the nagging feeling that she was being watched wherever she went, she'd dug out Zach's profile, ready to settle down in a quiet place that was off the beaten path.

She'd figured Zach must have already found someone. But he hadn't. And he'd seemed pretty close to perfect. Thus began their online chats and her eventual plans to join him as Catherine Tidsdale.

Fresh start.

Now she was here—in Blueberry Springs with a new life. New baby. New husband. New hair. New name. New curves—thanks to the pregnancy, as well as stress eating. New everything.

She owed nobody a thing, and vice versa. She'd

get up this morning, find a job, pay her own way in this relationship, and make it clear that neither she nor Zach should ever expect more than she could give.

Except that apparently half the town had already sent over baby items for Xavier, the bassinet having only been the beginning. Everyone was so kind and so giving it made her ill. She couldn't owe this many people. She had been raised knowing that if people brought you something it was never out of the goodness of their hearts, it was because tomorrow or the next day they'd be on your doorstep with their hand out, implying you owed them.

Catherine reached for the diaper bag, patting its hard plastic bottom, which was covered with cloth. Feeling along the edges, she could make out the faint outline of the extra passports she'd had made as a precaution. The bag's plastic handle was still heavy with the cash rolled up inside. It would be a trick and a half to retrieve it, but the money was safe. Just like the disguise she had at the ready in the zippered compartment inside. It wasn't much, just a wig, different shirt and a large scarf she could drape over herself to look pregnant if Xavier was in his baby sling, which also never left the bag. As long she had this and Xavier they could run at any moment.

She inhaled slowly, trying to calm her sense of unease.

The town meant well and she wanted Xavier to grow up in a place where people cared about their neighbors. She could handle their generosity. It was unlikely they expected more than she was willing to give in return. Most of the real world was not like her family. And if she had judged poorly and had chosen the wrong town, she had her exit papers.

Xavier began to stir, and out of habit, she lifted him before he could cry. She fed and changed him before heading downstairs to see what awaited her.

There, in the kitchen, wearing a white-and-blue-striped apron and flipping pancakes, was Zach.

She drew up short. She had not expected Mr. GI Joe to wear an apron, let alone make pancakes, which, judging from the ingredients still out on the counter, were from scratch. Then again, she supposed, like a good mother, the army had instilled good habits. She'd bet he was great with an iron and could make a bed without a single wrinkle.

She found herself smiling at the domestic scene before her, wondering if he was truly as amazing as he appeared.

"Do you eat pancakes?" he asked. He'd been humming what sounded like an old show tune, but

49

stopped, obviously having sensed her presence despite having his back to her. "I figured if you like Italian you must not mind gluten."

"I'll eat anything," Catherine said gratefully, her stomach rumbling at the scents of coffee, pancakes and bacon. A pink baby swing had appeared overnight, sitting where the bassinet had been beside the table last night. No, that had been lunchtime.

"What time is it?" she asked, while she burped Xavier. "And I'll cook tomorrow. What time do you get up?"

"It's a little before seven, Mountain Standard Time. I usually get up at five thirty, and I don't mind cooking."

Wow. She'd really slept. She'd gone for a rest after the spaghetti, waking only a time or two when Xavier was hungry, but all in all…she'd slept for almost seventeen hours.

"Is there anything *you* don't eat?" she asked as she put Xavier in the swing, securing the safety straps. She was either going to have to get up earlier than usual to cook when it was her turn, or the two of them would have to cook and eat separately. "Maybe we should eat on our own in the mornings."

Zach ignored the comment as he slid a pancake

onto the empty plate beside her. It was the same spot she'd sat in last night and she realized she had a place at this man's table. Her place. And he was feeding her. Making her breakfast.

She liked it. It made her feel warm, welcome and... "Where did this swing come from?" she asked, avoiding the unfamiliar and pleasant sensation that was swirling inside her.

"Turns out we're a bit of a gossip piece at the moment. There's even more stuff in the living room."

"More?" How was she going to keep track of what went back to whom?

Zach's expression was unreadable as he settled across from her, stacking three pancakes and drowning them in syrup.

"Gossip?" she asked.

"Yup." He cut through the pile, then shoved a big bite of pancake into his mouth.

"I suppose marrying someone you've never met and having her show up on your doorstep with a baby is noteworthy." She forced herself to sit upright, to not slump into a dejected mess. So much for keeping a low profile. She was in hiding! Didn't they get that?

As long as nobody started plastering her face on social media. Facial recognition could rat her out in a heartbeat if anyone from her family was actually looking for her in order to issue payback for their time behind bars.

Zach smiled at her dry comment, his blue eyes twinkling with amusement and what might even be happiness. The ridiculousness of the situation made her want to smile, too, as if they were sharing an inside joke that the world didn't understand.

But she could still feel the panic tightening, the lack of control she had over the way things were unrolling before her. She ignored the temporary sense of unease and settled on enjoying having someone with her in this lonely inner circle, if only for a moment or two.

"The town is mostly harmless," Zach said, polishing off his stack of pancakes.

She nodded, focusing on doctoring up her own, laying a few pieces of bacon on top before pouring syrup over it all.

Would a small community such as this one allow her to leave her past locked in the closet? Would they judge her for wanting privacy?

"Is anywhere in town hiring? I should get a job."

"You're ready to leave Xavier?" Zach asked, his eyebrows jumping up in surprise.

Catherine bit her bottom lip, glancing at her son in the borrowed swing. She hated to, but she couldn't just sit here and be dependent on Zach. "I need my own money. I was hoping I might find something I could do from home." She cleared her throat, feeling odd calling his place home. "From here."

"You know it's okay to lean on me for a few months," Zach said, his voice low and careful. "I don't expect much. Just help out here and there and we'll call it even." He gave a warm chuckle. "We are married, after all."

"I'm used to being independent." She knew that sounded formal, but she needed him to know she wasn't here to sit around and leech off of him.

"I can respect that," he said after a long moment.

"I do appreciate your kindness," she added quickly, feeling as though she'd been rude.

"I can ask around about jobs. What can you do?"

"I'm a fast learner. I can do anything."

"Drive a snowplow?"

"I'm sure I can learn." She was willing to figure out how to do anything. Even if it might lead to her freezing to death. "On second thought, maybe not that job."

"We'll find you something," Zach said. "Folks in town like to be helpful."

"It sounds as though it is a very kind place."

"The best." Zach leaned forward, circling his left hand in front of his nose as he said, "If you can handle them right up in your face."

She laughed at his act, making Xavier jump, and she realized it wasn't a sound her son was used to. He let out an uncertain cry, but Zach reached out, automatically hushing him while giving the swing a small nudge.

"You're good with kids." A thought struck her. "Do you have some?"

He shook his head, explaining, "I used to babysit for the lady next door. She had seven kids in the end, but Martha was the last one I sat for before heading off to join the army. Two more came after I left."

"The army?" He'd mentioned it in passing and Catherine wanted to know more.

"Yup. I was in just about everything by the end. I retired about a year ago."

"And how is civilian life treating you?" she asked.

Zach let out a huff that she took to mean that he wasn't so impressed with it.

"I suppose it takes some getting used to? Not having to bounce a coin off your bed every morning, and there being nobody around to shout at you." She straightened in her chair. "That's why

you got married! You need someone to yell at you."
She fell against the chair back, hands clutching her
stomach as she laughed.

Zach scowled at her and rocked the startled
Xavier some more. "I have enough people shouting
in my life, thank you. Try ignoring Liz Moss-Brady
on Main Street when she's heard a bit of gossip
that involves you. She'll shout and chase you down
until you finally acknowledge her." His smile was
wry, his eyes filled with an affection for the
woman, which told Catherine that maybe Liz and
civilian life weren't that bad in his books, after all.

"YOU DIDN'T TELL me she was this cute," Logan
whispered to Zach, catching his attention. Zach's
friend was peering around the kitchen archway,
watching Catherine's animated expression as she
tickled and hummed an old Frank Sinatra song to
her son, while changing him in the living room.

Zach adjusted the neck of his shirt, not liking
how tight it felt. He also didn't like his friend
checking out his wife. Even though she was still
basically just an acquaintance.

"It makes sense you ordered her online, you
know."

"You make our arrangement sound..." Zach

55

paused, unable to express all the ways Logan's words annoyed him, without punching the man. "She's not an object. She's a person. A mother. Someone's daughter. A real living human being with wishes and dreams. And wants."

"And does she want you?" Logan asked with a sly smile.

Would she want him?

And why did he find himself wondering? It didn't matter.

He scrubbed his face with a hand. Logan was getting to him. He needed a topic changer. He glanced at what Logan was wearing—a striped, knitted sweater. But the stitching was uneven, the hem crooked.

"What's this? Ginger learning to knit?"

"Annabelle." His daughter.

"Ah. Hence the stripes?"

"Hence the stripes." The normally well-dressed man grimaced slightly as he looked down at his sweater before letting out a soft chuckle. "Not bad for her first attempt, actually."

"Pretty good," Zach admitted. A sweater was a big first project to undertake, and he was confident he couldn't best her results.

"Good ol' George from next door saw me coming in and asked if she'd make him one, too."

"Nice of him."

"I just mean with you not able to find love on your own and Ginger striking out," Logan began, returning to the topic of Zach and Catherine.

"I'm not looking for love," Zach said quickly.

"Exactly. Companionship. She's perfect. You both need a warm body to talk to and keep each other sane."

"You make me sound unstable."

"I know how tough it is," Logan said, his voice lowering, his dark eyes serious. "Leaving the service and learning to trust people. It's not easy letting others in and being genuine, without having some sort of overriding top secret agenda driving every thought and action."

Zach let out a breath. He'd never talked about this with Logan, having assumed the man had transitioned without effort, easily doing all the things he'd mentioned.

"Think of this marriage like training wheels," Logan continued. "She needs a man to help support her while she gets settled somewhere new, as well as get her motherhood ship off the ground—or so I assume. And you need to learn how to let people in. All the way in. You know, so you feel all that emotional stuff we learned to keep under lock and key and behind an iron gate."

"Training wheels."

"Yup. Kind of like being a teenager all over again," Logan said, with a grin that made Zach's gut twist. He hadn't had that much luck in high school. He hadn't quite known how to take a girl's interest into something more than shy smiles or quick and awkward conversations. He'd been on dates, of course, but had never managed to find a relationship that had developed into something that left him brokenhearted when it ended.

Zach peered around the corner, watching Catherine. She'd started to make herself at home in small ways, leaving a stack of diapers on the main floor for changing Xavier instead of running back up to her room. When she was with her son, her guarded expression vanished, revealing just how closed she was with Zach. She was friendly, polite, but didn't act as though she was comfortable or truly open with him. Not by a long shot.

Logan had moved back into the kitchen and was leaning against the counter, arms crossed. He had his eyebrows raised in question, as though asking Zach if he'd made any progress with figuring out Catherine and why she was really here.

"So? Is she on the run?" he asked, when Zach didn't take up the conversation. "Want me to do a background on her yet?"

"No."

"You sure?"

"Yes."

Logan nodded thoughtfully. "I suppose if she'd been sent to silence you—you know, erase all that important, highly-sensitive, secret knowledge you have rattling around in your top paddock, she would have done it already." He brightened and smoothly turned to the doorway as Catherine entered the room with her son. "How's that little Xavier dude? Ready to learn how to snowmobile yet?"

"I'm not even going to humor you with a reply," she said.

"That sounded like one. So that would be a yes for next year?" He winked at Zach. Logan and Catherine had hit it off immediately, already making digs like long-time friends. Maybe it was the England-Australia connection. Union Jacks and Queen Elizabeth. Whatever it was, Zach had to admit he was a tiny bit jealous.

Something Logan had obviously noted, as he mouthed behind Catherine's back, *"She likes me."*

Zach scowled, causing his friend to grin and cozy up closer to Catherine. He swept Xavier from her arms. "Babies love me."

Xavier's bottom lip trembled, the move spreading to his chin before he finally let out a wail.

"Actually, they don't," Zach said. "You're too much of a dingo." He carefully plucked Xavier from Logan before Catherine could, determined—thanks to his testosterone—to one-up his friend as well as impress the woman in his life by settling the infant. Which he did.

He shot Logan a smug look, not caring if Catherine saw him or not.

"He likes Zach," she said, smiling warmly at her son. Zach wanted that smile aimed at himself. He bet it felt wonderful to be looked at like that. To be cherished and loved.

Wait. Now he was envious of an infant?

As though she was catching herself, Catherine's expression became more closed. She struck Zach as being very British as she said in a clipped tone, "You two have known each other a long time?"

"Too long," both men replied at once.

"And you work together?"

"Unfortunately," Zach said, as Logan added, "Bad decision on my part."

Catherine dug her child from Zach's arms. "We should let you work."

"We're fine," Logan said. "It's not every day Zach gets married. Are you guys going to throw a party?"

"A party?" Catherine asked. "Why?"

"Because we got married," Zach said. The last

thing she probably needed was the town fawning over them more than they already were. He had a feeling it might cause her to freak out. She needed time to adjust, settle in.

"Lots of time to think about it," Logan said. "Folks in Blueberry Springs love this kind of stuff. They might even throw a surprise one if you don't plan it yourself."

"They wouldn't dare," Zach said, dismissing the comment. He wasn't so involved in the community that they'd go to the bother. Logan was probably just angling to get Catherine to buy a dress from his wife's bridal shop.

"You wouldn't happen to know someone who's looking to hire an employee who can do some work from home?" Catherine asked.

Logan met Zach's eye and Zach shook his head. Nope. Not happening.

"Are you good with numbers? Well organized?" Logan asked.

"We should work on that new system for Mandy," Zach said, angling himself in front of Logan, pressing into his physical space, pushing him from the room as well as the conversation. "She needs it set up by Friday."

"I am," Catherine said, following them.

"Do you have experience with invoices—

sending them out, making deposits and the like? Communicating with customers?"

"Yes." There was cautious hope in her tone, and Zach wanted to punch Logan for leading her on.

He continued to press Logan. "Catherine can start looking for work in a day or two—once she's gotten over the jet lag. I'm sure we can help her find something."

"Like being our office manager. Both you and I suck at doing all that client billing. We've got a ton of people we've never even invoiced."

"I'm getting to it, and we don't suck at it."

"Did you ever charge Moe and Amy for redoing their locks in the middle of the night? Or installing their new system?"

"I'm getting to it," Zach said darkly.

"Right. I'm pretty sure there's a statute of limitations on billing." He leaned around Zach. "When can you start?"

"Right now?" she asked.

Zach gave Logan a look of warning.

"Our clients are waiting," Logan sang.

"They can keep waiting. Catherine needs a chance to settle in."

And he needed a chance to find her a job. One where she wouldn't be in his business, noticing things. Like how he could dream up complex security systems that could keep thieves out of federal banks. Things that would prove he wasn't just some regular joe, but a man with a past she might find threatening. A man who could break or hack his way into anything, anywhere, anytime. Because he had a feeling that if he wanted a chance with this woman, he needed to act as nonthreatening and normal as boring George next door.

4

*Z*ach had managed to coax Catherine into taking a walk. He hoped it would help ease their mutual feeling of being at loose ends, their conversations awkward as they danced around a day of domesticity together. As well, Xavier had become more and more unsettled as the afternoon wore on, so Zach had bundled the new arrivals in his extra winter wear. The baby had quieted after a block or two, and now they walked in silence, other than the quiet crunch of snow beneath their feet on the sidewalk.

Success.

Well, except Logan had promised Catherine a job. Why? She was running from something, and for all they knew she may have swindled money from her last boss. Plus while having them both work from home would normally be ideal for a young family, it was maybe not so ideal for two people who had just met, and had yet to determine if they enjoyed spending extended lengths of time together. Or any time at all.

"Do you want to see about getting some winter clothes?" Zach asked Catherine. She was pushing the stroller, her tousled mass of blond curls set off by the red-and-black plaid of the insulated jacket she'd borrowed. His big black mitts looked ridiculous on her slender hands, but seeing her dressed in his clothing made him feel warm inside. "There are a few stores a couple of blocks over."

Catherine blinked and inhaled.

"You can pay me back later if that's an issue," he said, guessing the source of her hesitation. She'd been careful not to overstep, and to keep a boundary between them. She was fiercely independent and he was curious as to what had made her that way. It caused him to want to take care of her, to ease the burden of always being in charge. Which was ridiculous, because that would be the last thing a woman like her would ever want.

"Or, honestly," he said, lowering his tone so it sounded a bit more grave, yet playful, "I should pay for it, since I brought you all the way across the planet to this freezing mountain town."

Catherine laughed as she shivered, hunching

further into his jacket. "You might owe me for that."

A few flakes of snow fell from the clouds, floating toward them. "We should have chosen Cyprus."

"But then we wouldn't have had this amazing winter wonderland."

"You lived along the coast?" He was fairly certain Cyprus got snow in the mountain regions.

She gave a nod of agreement, then tipped her face to the sky while letting out a huff of joy as the flakes drifted onto her pink cheeks. "This is incredible."

"You've seen snow before?"

"Of course, but this is…this is winter. *Real* winter. And technically, it's still only autumn. This weather will freeze you without a second thought."

"That's rather grim." Zach shoved his hands deeper into his pockets, having forgotten his own gloves while bundling up her and Xavier.

"Sorry," she said with resignation. "I'm like that sometimes."

"I have my moments, as well. 'The world is too much with us.'"

At the quote, Catherine's spine straightened and she looked at him with interest.

"Bob Dylan?" he mused, trying to recall who he

should attribute the line of poetry to. "No, Henry David Thoreau. Nope, that's not right, either."

"William Wordsworth."

"Ah yes. The cynical old bugger. If he could only see us now. His criticism of materialism and modernism. Man, he must be turning over in his grave faster than a hot dog on one of those rotisserie things at the gas station." Which wasn't that fast, now that Zach thought about it.

He was trying too hard to impress her.

"You like poetry?" she asked.

He hesitated, struggling to come up with a line or two that wasn't trite and overused—or a limerick he'd learned in the army that wasn't completely inappropriate to recite in front of a woman. One you wanted to like you, at least.

"I know a little of this," he said casually, "a little of that."

She quoted a line he didn't recognize.

"Shakespeare?"

She gave him a look loaded with disappointment.

Wrong. Not the old bard then.

"I memorized enough poetry to keep the ladies happy—in other words, impressed." He'd found he needed his memory banks for more vital information, like how to survive in enemy territory.

"Interesting," she said, sounding very proper and British as she teased him. "A ladies' man?"

"Not especially. I lacked..." He squinted, as though trying to see whatever it was he failed to possess so he could describe it, claim it, fix it.

"Follow through?" she asked in amusement.

Man, he loved the way she spoke.

"I was preoccupied maybe." With survival. Keeping himself together. Both in high school and later in life. "If you're afraid, don't do it. If you're doing it, don't be afraid."

"Is that a personal motto?"

"Genghis Khan. I'm not sure I agree with the first part. I say do it even if you're afraid, otherwise you'll never do anything worthwhile."

She nodded thoughtfully, her footsteps slowing as she peeked in on her bundled son to ensure he was protected from the flakes which were growing fatter, causing an almost-whiteout.

"Where did this *renaissance* man grow up, that he can quote Wordsworth and Khan, has a home security system that could rival Fort Knox, and isn't a big fan of winter conditions, since he thinks Cyprus is better than this? Florida? I've heard it's lovely."

"Philadelphia," he replied. "I actually don't mind winter here in the mountains. The cold is worth it. Although sometimes it goes on too long. There are other things I'd like to do than shovel the walk every day."

Zach nudged Catherine, pointing for her to turn right. The snow was falling harder now, but he knew from his short time in the mountains that the sudden flurry could be similar to a cloud burst, only with inches of fat flakes piling up instead of rain. The stroller was already having issues with its small wheels, the wet snow clumping as it collected on the sidewalk.

"Isn't the house the other way?" Catherine asked.

"We're a block from Wally's Sporting Goods. Let's let this weather finish whatever it wants to while we see what Jen can do to get you two geared up for a true mountain winter."

"Fur-trimmed parka?" Catherine asked hopefully.

"Boots so big and warm you'll have trouble walking."

She gave a shiver. "That sounds wonderful. Maybe add some snowshoes and a Saint Bernard dog with a little barrel of brandy attached to its collar."

"That I can arrange."

Catherine smiled up at him, happy and free, and he wondered if this was what real life looked like.

CATHERINE COULD SEE the shop up ahead, its promise of warmth like a beacon to her toes, which had gone numb about two blocks back. Her hands, despite the bulky mitts, were starting to ache from the cold. A few more seconds of brisk walking and they'd be there. Just a little farther.

Zach stopped, then backtracked a few steps. He stooped, brushing the snow near his large boot with his bare hand. As he straightened, he focused on something cupped in his palm. With his index finger, he pushed and poked, knocking off clumps of snow, until he held up something pinched between his fingers.

"How are you not freezing?" she asked, stomping her feet.

"Look what I found." He still wasn't walking, and Catherine checked on Xavier, who seemed warm and content. Maybe he was actually as frozen as she was, but the shock of it was preventing him from crying. Zach was still standing there as though expecting her to come over. She glanced toward the Wally's Sporting Goods sign. So close. And yet so far.

As she struggled with the stroller's wheels, which had done fine rolling over the hard crust of snow earlier but were now sticking in the new snow, Zach came forward, showing her his find. "A ring."

Up ahead, a woman as puffy as a penguin in all her outerwear exited the shop, a wave of heat shimmering in the air before the door swung closed again.

"It looks old," he said, walking slowly beside Catherine.

She wished he'd pocket it so they could move faster. The delightful flakes from earlier were now stinging her cheeks with a relentless cold.

She glanced at the ring when he held it her way. Her best guess was that it would be valued in the ten- to twenty-thousand-pound range. A nice find for sure.

Zach clutched it in his fist. "It's likely an heirloom and means a lot to someone." He shoved his free hand into his pocket and pulled out his phone. He kept stopping, then walking, then stopping.

He jabbed at the screen with what must surely be frozen fingers, then held the device to his ear. Seconds later he said, "Scott, it's Zach. Any chance you've had a report of a lost ring?" He described the piece, listened a moment, then said, "Beth Reiter's grandmother from the nursing home? Yeah, I know Gran."

He pocketed the fist holding the ring.

It was easy enough to make it look like you

were doing the right thing and claim that you'd returned it to the likely ailing, memory-challenged woman, when in fact you'd pawned it. Catherine sighed, confident about how this story was going to play out. People didn't do the right thing these days. They didn't return things if they didn't have to.

She adjusted Xavier's cap, wishing he could grow up in a world where people were honest even when nobody was looking. Where they shared the same values that she strived to hold dear. Old-fashioned, sure, but how wonderful it would be to be able to count on others. She had hoped, when choosing Zach and this small town, that Blueberry Springs was a place still stuck in its ways where morals were concerned. But maybe that kind of community no longer existed. Maybe they shared hand-me-downs, but that was all.

Zach ended the call and Catherine felt the urge to sigh as a way to release the disappointment welling inside her.

"Shall we? You look half-frozen." He guided her into the sporting goods store.

The shop was expansive and warm, stuffed with everything from cross-country skis, skates and sleds to big puffy jackets that looked so comfy she wanted to curl up in one even though it wouldn't have the comforting smell of Zach's cologne.

"Zach! How'd those skates work out for you?" called a welcoming female voice through the racks of bulky clothing.

"Pretty good."

A woman with a big smile appeared, her nose gem twinkling under the lights. Her blond hair was natural, unlike Catherine's, but had a funky streak of purple.

"Jen, this is Catherine and Xavier."

Catherine slipped off Zach's oversize mitts and smiled.

"They need outfitting for winter. Catherine, this is Jen Kulak. She owns the place."

Jen worked her gaze over the three of them, still smiling, then said, "I'd heard you'd gotten married, but said I'd believe it when I saw it." She stretched out a hand to shake Catherine's.

"Why is the place called Wally's?" Catherine asked.

"He's the old owner. Retired. Now it's all mine." Jen gave a playful cackle and rubbed her palms together as though she was an evil villain who'd finally gained the upper hand. "Mine, I say."

Zach let out a sigh as though unimpressed. "Anyway, I was thinking a proper parka. Ski pants. Hat. Everything."

"Right." Jen sobered up, even though a hint of

mischief was still gleaming in her eyes. "Let's start with Xavier."

She led them to a rack and started tugging out little snowsuits that she claimed would work in a car seat. "This brand kept my son warm. By the way, did you get the infant seat I sent over? Rob said he was going to deliver it, but when I checked the car an hour later it was still in there."

"He dropped it off before our walk," Zach said.

"Thank you for the loan. It's very generous," Catherine added.

Jen shrugged. "We aren't planning on having more kids. I'm just sorry our little snowsuit would be the wrong size for Xavier."

"You have just the one child?" she asked.

"Just the one." Jen had moved to adult sizes and was building a stack on a bench nearby.

"I'm sure we don't need all of this…" Catherine said uncertainly.

"You will," Zach stated, with a sureness that made her reassess the pile. How were they going to carry this home? And how much was it going to cost? Was the offer to work for Logan and Zach a real one? She could tell Zach hadn't been comfortable with it. She wasn't sure if he had something to hide—finances had always been a private and somewhat touchy subject in her family—or if he just didn't want her underfoot.

Jen was holding up items in front of Catherine. "Red okay?" she asked. "It would look amazing with your complexion."

"Mitts, not gloves," Zach said to Jen, adding black ones to the pile and removing a pair of thick gloves.

"Mittens? For me?" Catherine hadn't realized they were for adults as well as for children.

"They're generally warmer," Zach said.

"Just a bit unwieldy," Jen added. "But for your first winter, mitts are probably best."

The bell over the door jingled and a woman hustled into the store, her auburn curls coated with white flakes that quickly melted, giving her a sparkly appearance. "Zach!"

The urgency in her voice had Catherine turning to take a second look.

"I can *not* believe it!" the woman said. "I *swear* I thought Logan was a big fat liar!"

Zach inhaled slowly as though about to deal with a younger sibling. "Catherine, this is Ginger. Logan's wife. I'm sorry."

"Sorry?" Catherine gave him a questioning glance before being enveloped by Ginger.

She squeezed Catherine, her scent like the outdoors, then held her at arm's length. "You're British. Of course! It's perfect. Why didn't I think of finding Zach someone British?"

She released her grip.

"This is Xavier," Zach said, turning the stroller so Ginger could see Catherine's son. He was bundled in a thick layer of blankets, making Catherine feel like an ill-equipped mother. She fussed over her son. He was warm enough like this outdoors, but it was embarrassing not to have him dressed in proper winter attire.

"He's adorable." Ginger took in the child with a sweep, then turned to Zach once more. "A single mom, you scallywag. I can't believe you two met and married online. I thought Logan was pulling my leg. And you're so pretty..." She turned to Catherine again. "Why would you ever agree to marry this guy, sight unseen?" She slung an arm around Zach with an affection that told Catherine more about the man than any of Ginger's words.

The woman had quieted, watching her, waiting for an answer.

Catherine opened her mouth to reply to what she had believed was a rhetorical question, but couldn't summon anything to mind other than Zach's Genghis Khan quote. "'If you're afraid, don't do it. If you're doing it, don't be afraid.'"

Zach chuckled and gave his puzzled-looking friend a shrug before sharing a smile and a wink with Catherine, making her feel as though she was sharing a secret with him. Was this their first inside joke as a couple? Or rather, as friends?

"It's not love yet. But I like what's going on here." Ginger looked at the two of them. "It'll soon be something more. Quote me on that."

She focused on Catherine again, who turned her attention toward the stack of thick, insulated pants Jen had waiting for her to try on.

"Team Waffles or Team Pancakes?" Ginger asked her.

"What?"

"Oh, I do love your accent." She tried to imitate the roll of her 'a' and failed. "I'm a sucker for accents. It's what drew me to Logan—my husband. He's Australian. So dreamy."

"Speaking of dreamy, this is Rob. *My* husband." Jen put her arm around the waist of a man who had come to join them from one of the back rooms.

"I'm dreamy now, am I?" he asked, looking at her in amusement. "I thought I was His Holy Major Hotness."

"That, too." Jen went up on tiptoes to give him a kiss. And the way she smiled up at him, her body snug against his, made Catherine wistful. She wanted that. She didn't dare dream of having it for herself, but it looked absolutely wonderful.

ZACH WISHED Catherine would hurry up and finish shopping. She'd be diligently trying things on, ignoring the conversations and banter around her, and then something would catch her attention and she'd drift off, watching Jen and Rob, or get swept back into conversation with Ginger.

If he and Catherine weren't careful they were going to end up with their social calendar booked solid for the next week. And Zach didn't particularly want to have a social calendar at the moment. He had to figure out this whole husband thing and what his exact role was before they started going out on the town as Mr. and Mrs.

"Come on, join us," Ginger begged. "It's just a little birthday party for John. We're pretending it's an intervention, but then we'll surprise him with cake."

"He'll never fall for it," Zach said. Then added for Catherine's benefit, "John Abcott's a lawyer. And the townsfolk are always throwing surprise parties." He added again for Catherine, "The town likes to throw them as they had a really successful one a few months back."

"Please?" Ginger said. "It'll be a great way to introduce your new little family to the community."

Jen nodded.

"It's not a bad idea," Rob offered.

"We're not a…" Zach glanced at Catherine, who was looking as uncomfortable as he felt. Yes, legally, he supposed they were a family, and yet he didn't feel as though he'd earned the right to call Catherine and her son that. "It's a bit soon. Catherine's exhausted. The jet lag is crazy."

"Everyone's going to show up at your door," Ginger warned.

She was likely right. If they didn't appear in public, the public would come to them.

"It might be a good idea," Catherine said tentatively. "We could pop over for a minute or two?"

Zach could see the pros and cons of going to the party, but the smudges under Catherine's eyes were darkening despite the long sleep she'd had last night.

"You've only just arrived," he said, knowing he was pleading.

"It's been about twenty-four hours," Jen said with an amused smile.

"They're going to ask us if we're planning a reception," Zach warned Catherine.

"They expect a wedding reception?" she asked in surprise.

"What a grand idea!" Ginger exclaimed, clapping her hands together. "I have the perfect dress in my shop and a tiny tux that would be *so* adorable on Xavier."

"Whoa," Zach said, calming Ginger. "Easy, girl. There's no need for us to have a big party of any sort."

"You're a real killjoy, you know that?" she retorted with a scowl.

"Speaking of parties, when does this birthday party start?" Catherine asked, changing the subject and making Zach like her all the more.

"In ten minutes if you want to be there to yell 'Surprise!'"

"We don't," Zach said firmly, ushering his wife toward the cash register. Anything they hadn't already picked out could be purchased tomorrow.

"But yelling 'Surprise!' is so much fun. You never know if they're going to pee their pants or not," Ginger said.

Zach grimaced. The people he knew best tended to be a wee bit unpredictable when taken off guard. With special agents, their training tended to kick in and they went into self-protection mode, hand to their holster, or flipping over anyone who made the mistake of making body contact. Hardly a good way to start off a party. Although he doubted the nearing-retirement lawyer was armed or likely to otherwise defend himself when shouted at by a roomful of friends.

Zach slowly exhaled, realizing he was thinking like an agent, and not some boring regular joe.

"Fine," he said. "We'll come by in thirty minutes, and we're not staying a minute longer than twenty. Got it?"

"You're so cute when you get all tough and macho," Ginger cooed. "Doesn't he look cute with that red spreading up his neck?" she asked Catherine.

His wife's mouth curved up in mild amusement, but wisely, she began pushing her son toward the doors. Even though she obviously wanted to go to the party, she might be a keeper.

5

*B*y the time Catherine made it home, having shoved the stroller through the thick snow for blocks, she was a sweaty, tired mess. Her new parka, which reached her knees, almost meeting up with her high-on-the-calf winter boots, definitely did the trick keeping her toasty. She felt like she could hunker down and hibernate in this getup.

Zach, who'd tried to help despite her brushing him off, had carried the large bag of castoffs and extra winter items. Now, he battled the slippery armful as he tried to unlock the door, while keeping the bag out of the piled up drifts. It must have snowed six inches in thirty minutes. She'd never seen anything like it.

The snow had let up, but the heavy clouds

above looked as though there was plenty more to come. And she'd agreed to go out again. To a party. In a room filled with people she didn't know.

The town was great. She'd already decided that. It was very much what she was looking for in terms of raising Xavier. But it was a bit much with the enthusiastic welcomes. Okay, a lot much.

She was overwhelmed. But if she stayed home to catch her breath instead of going to the party, she was certain she'd be entertaining surprise visitors for days.

It was best to get it all over with now. Satisfy their curiosity about the newcomer so she could have some peace later in the week.

"Did Jen say she brought over a car seat?" she asked Zach.

"She did."

"And you have a car?"

"I do."

Catherine unzipped her coat and shoved her cap higher, off her forehead. The right gear obviously made all the difference when it came to staying warm.

"How's the parka?" Zach asked, the skin around his eyes creasing with amusement as he took in her overheated appearance.

"Perfect." And it would take weeks of part-time work to pay it off.

In time, she reminded herself. *In time.*

Zach swung the front door open and the bag in his arms escaped his grip, spilling its contents. He turned and picked up the stroller, child and all, and carried them indoors. Catherine hurried up the snowy steps and collected the blankets Xavier had been in, her new snow pants and Zach's borrowed jacket off the floor.

"Thanks," Zach plunked the stroller on the tiled floor of the entry. They were going to have a wet, slippery mess in here when all this snow melted. She had a feeling winter was going to be a lot of work.

Zach checked his watch, and she wondered if he was the last man their age who wore one, for practical reasons. "I'm going to run this ring over to Gran. Wanna come? She's a hoot."

"You're serious about not being there for the 'Surprise!' part of the party?"

"I said thirty minutes. We still have twenty."

It was tempting to stay home, to melt into a chair for a few minutes. But she also wanted to see what kind of man she'd married. Would he truly return the ring if she didn't go with him? Although who would say he was going to do something and then not do it?

Her brothers.

Uncles.

Father.

She sighed inwardly and rezipped her new coat. "I hope we're driving this time."

"We can drive," Zach confirmed. He stepped into the living room, collected the car seat and head to the garage. Catherine pulled Xavier from the stroller and followed him.

He was standing in front of a surprisingly small car, holding the seat by its top handle, making it look like a large picnic basket in his easy grip. He sucked one corner of his lips into his mouth in thought, then twisted to glance at her. "You have any idea how to install this thing?"

"I think so." She handed the bundled-up infant to him, gave Xavier an affectionate tap on his nose with the tip of her finger and opened the back door to the little Nissan. Somehow she'd expected the man to drive something larger. All the vehicles she'd seen on the roads so far seemed to be super-sized and sprawling, just like the local homes and yards.

She pushed the baby carrier across the bench seat. "In the middle is the safest," she said over her shoulder. Zach was lightly bouncing Xavier, trying to peer into the small space to watch what she was doing.

She took the long lap belt and twisted the infant seat so it rested backwards against the seat back.

She found the spot for the seat belt, clicked it in place, cinched it and awkwardly backed out again.

"Is that ball supposed to be in the green zone?" Zach asked, peering into the backseat.

"What ball?" She pushed her sweaty hair off her forehead.

"That leveling gauge on the side of the baby seat. The ball is in the red." Zach pointed to something that definitely looked like a safety device calling her installation efforts a failure.

"Here." Zach handed her Xavier and crawled in, banging his head on the roof as he went.

"Are you okay?"

"Peachy," he grumbled.

"Somehow I pictured you with a larger vehicle."

"It's in the shop being repaired. This is a loaner."

"What happened?"

"Needed a new bumper."

"What did you hit?" she asked.

He grunted as he adjusted the seat. "I didn't hit anyone."

"It was their fault then?"

"Everyone's fine," he said tersely.

"You don't want to talk about it?" she teased, testing his temper. Did he have a slow fuse or a quick one? What would he be like when he lost it?

"Not especially."

Was he embarrassed? That was kind of cute.

He backed out of the car a moment later, his face bright with triumph, the earlier hint of a temper gone. She handed Xavier to him again and crawled across once more to check his work. She gave the seat a good hard yank like she'd been taught to do. It moved.

"It's not tight enough. It shifted."

"Seriously?" He let out a grumble and passed her Xavier, trading places with her yet again.

This time he stuck a knee into the baby seat as he cinched the belt. "There. That's not going any-where. We're in the green. It's tight." He banged his skull coming out of the car and this time let out a quiet curse as he clutched his head. "Tell me we don't have to do this every time we want to go somewhere."

"No, there's a base that the carrier clicks in and out of." Her stomach dropped as she realized she didn't know where the base was. They'd strung the seat belt across the carrier instead. They'd done it incorrectly.

She groaned and refrained from releasing a few of her own curse words. She was overheating, Xavier was fed up with being handed back and forth and was starting to fuss. And they'd installed the seat all wrong.

"Where's the base?" Zach asked.

"I thought you babysat."

"There was no reason to drive the kids anywhere."

"The base," she said, as she squatted down to look more closely at the setup, "is connected to the carrier."

"So we disconnect them?"

"Maybe we should walk," she suggested.

"I never admit defeat to baby seats. We install the base, click in the carrier?"

She could hear him going into problem-solving mode and she relaxed, certain he would fix everything if she just stepped aside.

"Yes."

It was a nice feeling, being able to hand off this problem and all the frustration that went with it.

"What are you doing?" she asked. He had his phone out and was poking at the screen.

"I'm going to look up the manual online. It's time to get serious. Get this done right."

"You're searching for the manual?"

"Yes."

That was sexy. And it was definitely better than what had happened in the past, with the brand-new bookshelf she'd bought herself at age fourteen. Her determined father, meaning well as he helped her put it together, had instead destroyed it. He'd become certain that he was assembling it the correct way, and that the boards just needed a few more drill holes.

"You and I will not be bested by an infant seat," Zach promised. "Not today."

CATHERINE COULD TELL ZACH was feeling pretty pleased with himself as he drove them to the nursing home, Xavier secured in his car seat. It had been simple to install once they'd figured out how to do it. Although she had a feeling they were going to be later to the party than their thirty-minute promise.

"You don't give up easily, do you?" she asked as Zach pulled into the snowy parking lot outside a hospital and adjoined care center near the edge of town.

"Nope. All those hours sorting and untangling threads for my grandmother as she knitted, crocheted or did her needlepoint have paid off more than once."

"No way," Catherine said, delighted. "You were a sweet little towheaded boy sitting at the feet of your grandmother, tending to her yarn as she stitched?"

"Towheaded?"

"Blond."

"Oh. Yes. There was, however, a wee bit of protest."

"She must have been quite the woman. Wrangling you into essentially watching paint dry while she sat and stitched?"

"I can still hear her in my mind." His voice hit a higher, wobblier note as he spoke in a feminine voice. "'Zachary dear, quit fidgeting. The world needs more patient men.'"

"I'll agree with her there."

"Or 'The world will still be there doing the same old things in an hour. I need you here now.'"

"She was tough." Catherine watched Zach as he angled the car into a parking spot, noting the sureness of his grip on the wheel, the way his eyes darted to shoulder check and take a peep in his rearview mirror as he straightened the vehicle. He was strong, kind, patient and everything solid and good at first glance. All qualities she hoped her son would have.

"Even my first army commander wasn't as tough as she'd been. He was a little more direct and a bit less patient, though. 'Stick with the problem, Forrester, or I'll kick your...' Well, you get the picture."

Catherine smiled at the image of a commander ruling over Zach. "How long were you in the army?"

"It wasn't always the army, but that life kept me employed and fed since I was a teen."

"It suited you?"

"I thought so."

"But?" She could hear something in his voice.

"Aw, you know. The grass is always greener."

"Is it?" She was curious if he believed the expression to be true in his case.

He shrugged after turning off the engine, then gazed through the windshield as though mentally balancing out both sides. "When your daily work involves danger you begin to feel paranoid that your card's about to be punched."

"What do you mean?"

"When it comes to dodging death there are only so many times you can be lucky. Every time you play the odds."

She shivered at the thought of him facing danger, of the old arguments her parents used to have.

"But every time you play, the odds reset," she said quietly, quoting her father. He used to fight with her mother over how he could get caught embezzling, or whatever the crime de jour happened to be. It had amazed Catherine that they'd stayed together despite the fights. Most of the other men in the gang were in and out of marriages and relationships faster than anyone could keep track. It wasn't cheap, either. She'd seen more than one disgruntled ex-wife quieted with a thick envelope of cash to go spend on herself.

There'd been a time when Catherine had been proud of the way her parents had stayed together, knowing their marriage was unlike the others. Her father treated his wife like a queen, giving her the latest and greatest in cars, vacations, gems and jewels. And then one day, when Catherine was fourteen, she'd seen it for what it truly was. He'd been paying her off. Giving her a reason to remain quiet, to stay. Reasons other than love or devotion.

"They say the odds reset," Zach mused, "but overall you're still playing the same game."

That had been her mother's point.

"So you came home."

"I bowed out and started the business with Logan."

Because, as she'd discovered yesterday, he was alone. He had no home to return to after leaving active duty.

She struggled with the urge to reach over and touch his hand, to let him know he wasn't alone. Instead she kept her hands clasped in front of her and her gaze out the window at the snowy scene surrounding them.

On the radio the announcer called out the time. They were definitely going to be late for John's birthday gathering, but this felt worth it.

"You thought civilian life would be straightforward and easy?" she asked, referring to their earlier conversation.

"The idea of trading heavy problems for light ones was appealing, but it is an adjustment. The things I care about now are whether my neighbor is bothered by the weeds in my yard rather than whether my team is about to be weeded. If you know what I mean."

"Very poetic."

He smiled. "I try."

"I can tell." The way he was watching her caused a warm tug in her gut. She liked his easy charm and his contradictory serious undertone. His life hadn't been perfect, either, but he was still standing, still had a concrete backbone she felt she could count on.

"You're looking at me as if you just decided you might like me."

She laughed, feeling free, safe. "Is my expression that readable?"

He got that contemplative look again. "It's more like I know you." He added quickly, "I don't. But it's as though..." His blue eyes grazed her, searching for clues, things to put into words.

She knew what it was.

"There aren't many people like us." People with

a past so dark that even a floodlight couldn't illuminate it.

During the conversation they'd begun to lean in, their shoulders touching over the console, their lips now close enough that one of them could raise their chin and they'd be kissing.

"Maybe that's what it is," Zach said softly.

This close she could see the faint scar on his cheek, the pulse in his temple, feel the heat from his body. He smelled good. Like someone she could get close to.

She straightened, heart pounding. She opened the car door, letting a blast of cold air into the vehicle's warmth. Seconds later she was out in it, opening the back door to retrieve Xavier.

What had she been thinking? She'd almost kissed Zach!

She needed to stay distant, not hint that she had a darker-than-most past—although wasn't that obvious, due to the way she'd come running across the world after marrying a perfect stranger?

They weren't alike. He had dedicated his life to good things. To protecting others. To honor. He was a good man, and wouldn't understand that she wasn't like her family, who'd sold arms on the black market—the very thing most military men risked their lives to fight against in hostile areas of the world.

Managing to retrieve Xavier from the cramped backseat, she tried for a teasing tone as she met up with Zach alongside the car. "What's your real vehicle again, and when do you get it back?"

"A Land Rover. Tuesday." He was watching her, the slope of his slumped shoulders hinting at disappointment for the way she'd so quickly retreated.

"Ample rear seat?"

"For all things." The hint of flirtatiousness in his gaze made her blush. She wanted to flirt back. Desperately.

Instead, she handed him the carrier and flipped a blanket over Xavier, protecting him from the cold wind whipping across the parking lot.

In awkward silence they walked to the building, then down the long shiny hallways, every moment of quiet highlighting how she'd ruined their little moment, taken it and stomped on it.

"What's with the Team Pancakes or Team Waffles thing?" she asked. "Ginger asked me back at the store."

"No clue." Zach shot her a quick smile and knocked at a wide door, after setting down Xavier in his carrier. "Probably trying to figure out if we're compatible."

He held her eye until she had to look away.

From inside the room came a loud man's voice. "You gonna get that, sweet cheeks?"

Zach let out a chuckle.

"Which team are you?" Catherine asked, curiosity getting the best of her despite her vow to keep some distance between them.

"Depends on my mood."

"You're a pancake. All the way."

Zach's chin jerked as though he was insulted. He turned, leaning against the wall to face her more fully. "Pancake? I'll have you know that I'm complex enough to be a waffle."

Next, a woman's voice came from inside the room. "Reggie, don't be so lazy!"

"I'm being practical and conserving energy," the man replied. "The door's always for you, my social butterfly."

Catherine shook her head, ignoring the fight going on inside the suite. "*I'm* a waffle. You're about the essentials. No frills. That says pancake all over it."

"Frills, huh?" Shuffling sounds slowly grew louder on the other side of the door. Zach leaned toward Catherine, the fresh scent of snow following him. She caught a hint of his aftershave, which clung to Xavier's clothing after being held by him. She already associated the smell with good things like snowmen, hot cocoa and happiness.

Zach was still in her space and she forced herself not to step back, but to hold her ground.

"I like pancakes because they're quick and easy." His voice was low, with a hint of something in his tone that made her body respond in a way it hadn't to a man in nearly a year. "The problem is..." Oh, how his voice was delicious. "...syrup runs off of pancakes, it doesn't pool, so they're never quite sweet enough."

Catherine opened her mouth to retort, but the suite door opened and an elderly woman exclaimed with glee, "Oh, it's Zach!" She placed her hands on his cheeks, smiling up at him before frowning remorsefully. "How's the poor car?"

"I'm picking it up on Tuesday."

"I am sorry about that. I hope the bumper didn't cost too much."

"It's fine."

The woman's lips pursed and she shook her head. "I really wish you'd let me pay for it, since I was the one without insurance." She saw Catherine standing behind Zach and explained, "I no longer drive, but it was an emergency. And wouldn't you know it, I slid right into poor Zach's Range Runner."

"Land Rover," he said quietly.

"Yes, that big thing."

Catherine took a second look at Zach. So he

hadn't been embarrassed about the accident; he'd wanted to change the subject because he'd been protecting a little old lady? She wasn't sure what that meant, but it made her heart warm.

Catherine bent over Xavier's carrier to make sure he wasn't overheating, and the woman focused more closely on her. "Now who do we have here?"

"This is Catherine," Zach said, then cleared his throat as he lifted Xavier in his seat. "My wife, and her son, Xavier."

"Married! I thought that was just a rumor. Ginger said she hadn't found you anyone."

"This is Gran," he added.

"Everyone calls me that," she said, catching Catherine's uncertain expression. "No need to be related to have the honor." The woman turned back to the suite, hollering, "Reggie! Come meet Zach's new wife! He found someone." Reggie said something and she hollered back, "I'm not fibbing! It's true. She's standing right here with her baby! Get off your duff and come see." She turned again, all smiles. "What a sweet picture the three of you make."

Catherine awkwardly shifted from foot to foot, intrigued by how Zach didn't seem at all fazed by Gran.

Zach reached into his coat pocket. "I think I

found something that belongs to you." He pulled out the ring, and Gran peered at it for a moment as though trying to look through invisible reading glasses. Then her expression brightened.

"Reggie! Break out the good sherry! Zach found my mother's old engagement ring." She waved her hand. "Come in! Come in! That ring slides right off my finger in this cold weather. I need to get it resized."

"We're actually on our way to John's birthday party," Zach said, not moving. "I just wanted to drop this off so you could stop worrying."

"Oh, that's so sweet of you." Gran frowned. "John's party? Wasn't his birthday last month?"

"I'm not sure."

Her expression froze for a second before she said hurriedly, "Well, you'd better go. You can't be late. So nice of you to drop this off for me. Lovely meeting you, Catherine, dear."

The door closed and Catherine gave Zach a surprised look, to which he shrugged in reply.

The door opened again and Gran held out her hand. "Zach, dear, since I don't drive anymore and I never think to ask Mary Alice to drop me off at the jewelry store, would you be a dear and get this resized? I want to wear it to church on Sunday."

"Of course." Zach pocketed the ring again. "What size?"

"Just one down from that should be fine." And she shut the door again.

With no mention of a reward, and him willingly taking on another favor, Catherine fell a little bit in love with her helpful and honest husband.

———

As Zach pulled up outside the home where John was celebrating a birthday that surely numbered well into the sixties, he let out a sigh and rubbed his eyes. What Gran had said about the lawyer's birthday being last month seemed accurate. Was this a belated celebration?

Something felt off, especially with Gran giving them such a hasty goodbye, but he couldn't quite put his finger on it.

He used to be good at sussing out the reasons why stuff didn't add up.

"You're not a social animal, are you?" Catherine asked.

"It's going to be a zoo."

"We don't have to go in."

He appreciated the offer, but she'd been right earlier in suggesting it was best to get the curiosity over with, so they wouldn't be bombarded throughout the coming weeks. Maybe then he could get to the bottom of why she danced away whenever they seemed to connect. Oh, right. Because she was a widow who wasn't looking for love, or anything beyond companionship.

Like the goof he was, in the car he'd all but leaned in, eyes closed, lips pursed, even though she'd made it abundantly clear she wasn't interested.

"Do we have a story?" he asked, thinking ahead to the party and the line of questioning that would surely ensue.

"Oh, like a cover?" She wiggled in her seat, enthused by the idea.

"Yeah. Sure." The truth was, their unorthodox arrangement was a tad embarrassing, and he hoped to steer clear of any conversations that involved how they'd met or what had caused them to take the leap with a stranger. The good thing was that guys rarely asked those kinds of questions, and nobody but Logan knew that he'd married her and forgotten about doing so.

"What should it be?" Catherine asked.

"We met online."

She gave him a blank look and he grimaced. This was his thing—thinking on his feet and coming up with good cover stories. So why couldn't he?

Because he'd be lying to people he cared about.

He cared about the people of Blueberry Springs.

When had that happened?

A chill rippled over his flesh and his old commander's advice echoed in his ears. *"Don't get involved. You'll only put yourself and others at risk."*

Inhaling slowly, Zach unclenched his hands, reminding himself that there was no risk. Not any longer. He was doing the real-world thing now. No more dangerous cases, no more big secrets.

Just a woman with an infant who'd traversed the world to come live with him, because she was in mourning and wasn't in contact with her family —by choice.

That was a lame cover story, and after twenty-four hours together he should have more on her than that.

"And...?" Catherine prompted.

"Maybe it's easiest to tell the truth?" he offered. Although not all of it. He wanted her to see him as a regular guy, not someone to fear, someone with secrets, or a past that would surely make her uncomfortable around him.

"The truth?" she said, her voice hollow.

They were silent for a moment, and a burst of laughter filtered into the car from the house they were parked outside of. It was going to be loud and warm in there. Maybe it would be too much for Xavier and they could leave early.

"Maybe not the truth," he answered, thinking of

himself and the things he never planned to speak of, the stories he hoped Catherine would never ask him to tell.

"Everyone's going to want to know why I came over here."

"True love," Zach said, a hint of irony in his tone.

"And where Xavier's father is." A note of vulnerability had crept into her voice, and Zach reached for the keys to start the engine.

Catherine held out a hand to stop him. "Simon passed away when I was pregnant. I was alone, and so I came here, hoping for a fresh start and to give Xavier a family. That's the truth." She was so filled with sorrow that Zach did what he hadn't dared yet do, and he reached out to gently touch her cheek.

"I'm sorry about Simon."

A tear fell from her eye, and she quickly swiped at it. "I'm fine."

"I know you are. You're very strong, you know that?"

Catherine gave a huff of disbelief that sounded as if it came from a gut twisted with grief and remorse.

Maybe her cover story was just what she'd said it was and nothing more. He was so out of practice in dealing with genuine human emotion that he'd erroneously assumed there had to be more as a driver for her life-changing event. But maybe it was just grief pushing her to take the risk and come to Blueberry Springs. He knew that when it came to doing the unthinkable, there was nothing bigger than emotion as the reason behind it.

"Even though you're strong, it's okay to lean on me." He would be here for her, wouldn't he? He could make promises he never used to be able to make, for fear of suddenly having to vanish. "I admire that you want the best for Xavier, and that you're willing to take a risk to find that for him." Unsure what she was thinking, and what he should say to let her know that she could let down her guard, he added, "I can't give you everything, but maybe—"

"I don't want everything. I'm just looking for an honest, normal life."

"Me, too," he mumbled. "Me, too."

And never in his life had he wanted it more.

6

*A*s they entered the house, Catherine began to wonder what she had been thinking in saying yes to attending the party. The place was packed with people, noise and food. And as soon as they were safely inside the door, everyone turned and yelled, "Surprise!"

Catherine clutched Xavier's carrier, stumbling backward and landing against Zach, who caught her. With one smooth move he had her and the now crying child behind him, his stance wary and wide, as though ready to defend them. In her confusion she wasn't certain whether her heart was pumping that extra beat or two because of the way he was sheltering them, like they meant something to him, or from the shock of the unexpected greeting.

"Zach, you look as surprised as if you just gave birth to a camel!" A woman in a pink floral shirt with a booming smoker's laugh came over, and Catherine instantly disliked her. The woman thought this was amusing, taking them by surprise and making Xavier cry. She ought to be ashamed of herself.

Catherine took in the room with a sweeping gaze. Cake. Gifts. There was even a banner on the far wall that said Congratulations Zach and Catherine!

"How did they know we'd come?" she whispered to Zach. And how had they put this all together so quickly? She'd only arrived in town yesterday.

"I hate ambushes. Absolutely hate them." His neck was red and his hands were in fists, even though the rest of him had eased into a more casual stance at her side.

Raw energy was positively vibrating off him, and Logan had made his way out of the crowd to stand in front of them, his eyes glued to Zach's as he said, "Cool it, man. It's just a party. Just some people having a get-together."

Catherine bounced Xavier in his seat and shushed him as people mulled around them, offering congratulations, taking their coats, shaking hands and trying to take Xavier from her. While she was flattered by the thought and effort that had gone into the party, she already wanted to go home.

"Should have seen this coming," Zach muttered to her. There was something in his tone that was reluctant, self-disparaging, as if he was berating himself for not expecting the surprise.

"I think that would be missing the point." She wanted to chuckle at how much he simply hated this moment—even more than she did. People were still smiling, their eyes shining with glee for having secretly pulled off the party as well as gotten them there.

Zach glanced at Catherine, his blue eyes still narrowed as if he was holding a grudge. "I don't like having heart attacks."

"It's flattering they care."

"But not good for my well-being," he grumbled.

He reached for the diaper bag slung over Catherine's shoulder, but she gave a quick, "I've got it," and tightened her grip on its strap as well as the baby seat.

"Stand together," a woman commanded. She was wearing a blue floral blouse with a loud pattern that matched the camel-comment making woman's shirt. The sea of blue flowers waved at her as the woman raised her phone to take a photo. "I'm going to post this in the paper."

Catherine's blood chilled and she raised her hand from its spot on her bag's shoulder strap to hold it in front of her face, shielding herself, unable to speak for what felt like an endless moment. Finally finding her voice, she said loudly enough that the woman could hear, "I don't like having my picture taken. And I'd rather not be in the paper, thank you."

She had to leave. She needed to hide. Everyone here had cell phone cameras. Social media. Facial recognition. She'd be found in a heartbeat if her family was still looking.

She should have thought of this sooner. But she'd naively believed the party was in someone else's honor, and that her presence would be nothing more than a curious footnote.

The woman in the pink shirt was staring at her in disbelief.

"Please, I just don't want one taken." Catherine's tone was sharp, her voice quavering in poorly disguised panic.

"No pictures, please," Zach said smoothly, sliding between Catherine and the camera, while steering her in a new direction.

"Thank you," she managed to squeak, leaning into the shelter of his arms, Xavier's carrier bumping her leg.

"Do you want to leave?"

Her eyes teared up at the suggestion, but she shook her head. This was to be her new home. She had to stick it out, show her gratitude to the organizers and partygoers for all they'd done, as well as quickly build a reputation for being camera shy. It was the only way to be safe if she was ever going to belong to a community.

A woman came up and bent over Xavier. "Oh, he's adorable. Can I hold him?" She was already peeling back his blanket so she could reach the buckles to release him.

Catherine panicked. She wasn't ready to let go of Xavier, to allow him out of her sight in case she needed to run. She knew she didn't; she knew she was safe. But she couldn't seem to overcome the urge to pull the car seat away from the woman as she tightened her grip on the diaper bag slung over her shoulder.

"Whoa there, Gloria," Zach said smoothly. "Let's give Catherine a moment or two to settle in before we start mauling her child."

"Oh, Zach," the woman said. "I won't maul him. Amber and Scott are just taking their sweet time on the grandchild front and I need a dose of special time."

"Special time?" Catherine asked, almost fearing the answer.

"When you're our age and you hold a baby it

transports you back to that special time," a woman said, joining Gloria and smiling down at Xavier.

"When we were new moms and the world felt so full of potential," Gloria added.

As the crowd ebbed and flowed around them, Catherine noted how the women all seemed to have a special smile for Zach, the men almost reverent in a way that was different than the kind she'd seen reserved for her father. Men had approached her dad with an undertone of fear, sometimes so thick you could practically smell it coming off them. When she'd been small, he'd seemed invincible, crowds of people parting for him as they would for a king, a man in charge of the whole entire world and unable to do wrong.

Oh, but the wrongs he had committed...

As a man gave Zach an open, easy smile, shaking his hand and clapping him on the back, she could see that his respect was genuine.

Over the next several minutes Catherine felt as though she'd never said "hello" or "pleased to meet you" so many times in her entire life. Everyone was so delighted for her and Zach it was overwhelming.

He kept them in constant motion as they moved through the stuffy, crowded room, but finally he paused, ladling her a glass of nonalcoholic punch.

"This isn't so bad," she said under her breath.

Zach let out a huff of laughter as Catherine took a welcoming sip of the cool punch. She rocked Xavier's carrier, which she'd set on the floor, his blanket and snowsuit peeled back.

"I want to take him out of the carrier, but I fear I'll never get him back from the ladies if I do."

"Good call," Zach said.

She could see the unspoken questions in his eyes in regards to her mini freakout over having a photo taken. She was going to have to give him a story to explain it all.

"I… S-someone's stalking me," she stuttered, offering a partial truth. "I don't want pictures on social media. In case." She shut her eyes, knowing how slim the chance was that anyone in her family would come across the photos and track her down. But she'd made it clear she was no longer on their side, and the way they'd all ended up in jail, while she had walked, didn't look good. Even being related by blood wouldn't protect her if anyone was out for payback. "It sounds paranoid, I know."

He watched her for a split second, then, seeming to accept her excuse, lifted his punch glass to his lips. "Incoming gossips at your six o'clock," he murmured over its rim.

Before Catherine could move, the two women in the flowery blouses surrounded her, hemming her in against the table.

"Will the two of you be holding a reception?" asked the woman in the pink shirt. She'd been the one who'd made the camel comment earlier, and so far she was the one Catherine was most leery of. "I've offered to host a combined bridal and baby shower, and I'm sure Frankie would like to hold a little something for you, Zach—unless, of course, Logan has something planned." The woman paused for an answer, her expression expectant.

"Catherine has only just arrived," Zach said calmly, and Catherine found herself edging closer to his side.

The woman in the blue floral blouse—the earlier photographer—had obviously noted their physical proximity and was smiling, her cell phone still clutched in her hands.

"That is a very lovely gesture," Catherine said carefully, her mind awhirl with which approach she should take.

"It is?" Zach asked in surprise.

She knew how easily she could have an enemy in the blue lady for refusing to have her photo taken. She struck Catherine as the type who might quietly, yet publicly, begin to question Catherine's marriage motives behind her back. She could see how it would go. She was a woman who had married Zach sight unseen just so she'd have a father for her baby. It would be easy for the woman to socially ostracize Catherine, while cooing over poor Zach who had a heart of gold, et cetera, et cetera.

While Catherine wanted to be able to lie low and be left alone, she didn't want to bring sorrow or gossip to Zach's door. He deserved better. People respected him and it hurt to think that she might cause some of that to vanish.

"The town has been very generous, and very accepting," she said. "So kind and welcoming. Thank you."

The women smiled.

Catherine smiled back, confident she understood them. They were good people, well intended, but would circle the wagons around one of their own—Zach—to protect him. She just had to make sure, if they ever decided to circle, that as his wife she'd earned the right to be on the inside.

"Well, we'll plan something then," the pink-shirted woman said.

"Yes, something," Catherine agreed. Preferably a vague date in the future that would never come around.

From behind her she could catch snippets of conversations about her and Zach.

"She moved on rather quickly, don't you think?"

"How long has the baby's father been gone?"

"I wish I had the guts to take a page from the 1882 book on dating and mail myself off to some stud. But knowing my luck I'd get the town sleaze-ball instead of a real man like Zach."

There was laughter and Catherine felt her cheeks flush.

The woman in blue said, "I forgot to introduce myself. I'm Liz Moss-Brady, and this is my sister, Mary Alice Bernfield." She gestured to the woman in pink.

"Keep yourself free the Saturday after next," Mary Alice advised.

"Oh!" Catherine said in surprise. She wasn't expecting something so soon or definite. "Oh, we, um..." She looked to Zach for help, but his eyes were wide, as if he'd just seen his grandmother naked.

Yup. No help coming from him for the time being.

"I—we—only just arrived, and Xavier has been so colicky," Catherine said. "We really don't need something so soon. Please, don't put yourself out to arrange it so...quickly."

Both women were sizing her up again, eyes narrowed.

"Honey, this is Blueberry Springs," Liz said. "It's what we do."

"Nobody gets married around here without notice, or a party," Mary Alice said, gesturing to the roomful of people.

"We are already married," Catherine said carefully.

"And did you have a bridal shower back home? I heard you arrived with nothing more than that diaper bag and a backpack," Mary Alice said with a look.

"Right," Catherine said seriously. "I see your point. I simply don't want to overstep, or cause anyone undue stress with organizing something under such a tight deadline."

Both women gave a harrumph, as if she'd insulted their ability to throw something of this magnitude together in short order.

"Marriages, births and deaths are the biggest things to happen to our citizens, and we're all about celebrating milestones and welcoming newcomers," Liz said pointedly. She repeated carefully, "It's what we do."

Mary Alice locked her gaze with Catherine's, then reached into her blouse and pulled out what looked like a small tin. She opened it and offered it to her, never once breaking eye contact. She was smiling pleasantly enough, but it was clear—this woman and her sister were the alpha females in town. Possibly even the alpha everything, bears included.

The woman rattled the can and the room

seemed to grow a little quieter. She asked mildly, "Mint?"

"That would be lovely," Catherine said. She'd had worse from the bosom of her late grand-mother. This was at least in a sealed tin.

The people around them were silent as Mary Alice shook a mint into Catherine's outstretched palm. She pointedly placed it in her mouth with a smile. "Thank you."

"Bless her heart," someone murmured behind her, after which the room started buzzing again as chatter returned to its earlier levels.

"Keep that Saturday free, dear," Mary Alice said. "We're going to throw you two a reception."

ZACH FLOPPED into his computer chair and let out a deep sigh.

Well. That party had been something. The kindness and generosity had been a great welcome for Catherine, although definitely over the top. The poor woman hadn't been in town for more than a day and they were already surprising her with a shindig.

But what had really thrown him was Catherine's fear over having her photo taken. That had set off mental alarm bells and caused his agent senses to go on high alert.

She'd said she had a stalker. She was hiding.

He wanted to find out who it was and strangle the guy for causing her to fear having a normal life.

But despite the surprise of the party being for them, and then the panic over the photo, she'd stayed at the event. Had faced the town's biggest gossips and won them over. Except now they were having more parties to celebrate their platonic, companionable union.

He really hated those two descriptors.

Then again, he supposed the town threw parties for couples everyone knew wouldn't last a year. This wasn't that different. Although he hoped their marriage lasted longer than twelve months. It had been only a day and a half so far but he already liked having Catherine and Xavier in his life, and knew that if they left, his world would feel empty and lacking in purpose.

He stared at his computer screen. Catherine and Xavier had turned in for the night after what he and Catherine had dubbed The Battle of the Bath. It had been a wet one involving both of them, one very slippery infant and a poorly designed baby bathtub that he vowed they would never use again.

Zach had come into his office to do something, but he couldn't recall what it was.

How long before Catherine was ready for Xavier to have his own room and this upstairs office became a nursery?

Zach shook his head, subtly amused by his thoughts and new situation. A baby's bedroom. He hadn't seen that coming when he'd bought the house last year. It felt right, though, and he spun in his chair, imagining the space, the little touches he and Catherine would add. Well, he hoped she would allow him to add. Touches such as a giant plush giraffe standing in the corner. One big enough for Xavier to climb when he was older. Although maybe that wasn't safe. Maybe an animal closer to the ground, such as a giant panda, would be better suited for play.

He began looking for teddy bears online, then realized he should really be ordering a laptop for Catherine to work on when she was ready to straighten out the business's accounting.

Zach paused in his typing and leaned back in his chair.

He was keeping her, wasn't he? Already taking off the training wheels, letting her in, giving her a job despite the reservations he'd had earlier in the day.

She'd won him over. And why not? She was

strong as heck. Smart. Good with difficult people. And the two of them connected.

He thought of the moment in the car where they'd almost kissed, and how protective he'd felt when everyone had yelled "Surprise!" at the party, scaring her. That had been the worst part—not his own shock, but seeing her frightened. Then her panic at the idea of a photo being taken.

He began mulling that over again. A stalker.

As he allowed his mind to roll the problem over like a stone, he came up with a truth he felt all the way down to his toes.

She was hiding because this stalker was not your run-of-the-mill guy with a crush. He'd scared her. Maybe even enough to send her here to Blueberry Springs and marry a man she didn't know.

That was a lot of fear.

He twisted his chair to the left and snagged his phone off his desk, then texted Ethan Mattson, the one man in town who just might match some of his skills when it came to the tech world.

Hey, man. How good is facial recognition these days on social media?

Ethan replied, *Heard you got married. Worried she's going to find photos of you doing something stupid?*

Zach paused. Now that Ethan mentioned it...

Nope. Work reasons only.

Zach popped over to a website that sold toys

while he waited for Ethan's reply. He selected a stuffed giraffe for his cart. Just a small one. Then added a big fat hippo, as well.

I heard you're having a bachelor party? came Ethan's reply.

Nope.

His and hers wedding shower?

Nope.

You're not going to escape the town. You know that. I heard she already said yes.

Yeah. Why had she said yes? Not just to him, but to a reception. To a shower.

He typed out his reply, mulled it over, then hit Send. *I'm busy that day.*

Which day?

Whichever one they plan for.

They've caught you by surprise once already.

Zach grumbled under his breath. That they had. And he hadn't liked it. Neither had Catherine, which had made him like her all the more. The way she'd stuck to his side had warmed him from the inside out.

Had she said yes to the parties simply to get the town off their backs? Maybe she had a plan to keep putting off the reception until it never happened? That's what he'd have done if he'd been thinking.

They've already hired Lily to make sandwiches, Ethan texted.

They moved fast; Zach had to give them that. Lock everything in early so there'd be no ducking out.

Can she say she's double-booked and push them back a few weeks?

Why?

The town's going to scare off my wife. Zach paused, then backspaced over "my wife," replacing it with "Catherine" before sending the message.

She said yes, man. Women love a good fussing over.

But did Catherine? Zach hadn't really gotten that vibe from her. They'd connected because they had a similar, stand-back-and-watch approach to life. Slightly skeptical. And they jibed because they seemed to meet on a level that was normally left vacant by others.

Zach let out a sigh and typed *Please?*

So, facial recognition?

Ethan had to be yanking his chain. *Now* he wanted to talk about facial recognition?

What's the latest? he asked.

There was a long pause before Ethan's next text, and Zach started to believe it might be faster to do the research himself than to wait for the man to stop ribbing him about his marriage and answer the question.

Lily says she'll push the date back, but that you owe

her one for making her look like she can't read her own calendar.

Tell her I love her.

Ethan typed back an expletive and Zach chuckled. That man had it bad for his wife. That was good, but made it way too much fun for Zach to tease him by acting as though he had a thing for the cute and fiery woman.

Fine. Tell her thanks.

He could practically hear his friend give a disgruntled harrumph even though they were across town from each other.

Ethan sent another message, finally answering Zach's original question. *People can find each another with facial feature matching. It's slick. This mom in Argentina found her son a decade after he went missing based on facial recognition.*

Zach set his phone down and mulled over the implications for Catherine. She was smart to stay out of the public eye when it came to photos and the newspaper. But how was she going to do that forever? And who was this guy that was making her life miserable? Xavier's father? Was he actually alive? Or was it someone else?

Zach's fingers itched to start researching Catherine's ex, but he had no name, no fingerprints, no location and no legal access to a searchable database. He had nothing.

Where had the two met? Had it been a long romance or a short one? He wanted to know everything.

And it wasn't just his old training kicking in. It was more than that.

It was because he was starting to want things to be a bit like real life with Catherine, and he instinctively knew that what she held in her past might interfere with that dream.

CATHERINE HAD MADE BREAKFAST, surprising Zach, who had been moving his office to the basement, prepping the room for Xavier. Honestly, he could have waited another year, as she was far from ready to let her son out of her sight at night.

She'd made pancakes. Not frilly waffles. Just not-quite-sweet-enough pancakes. Zach hadn't said a word and she'd itched throughout the meal, waiting for him to say something so they could banter about who was on which breakfast team— waffles or pancakes.

Finally, while putting the dishes in the dishwasher, he'd said, "I can't believe you think I'm Team Pancake."

Yes!

"Because you are."

"And you want me to think you're Team Waffle? You don't even wear nail polish."

Okay, so that was true. She'd given that up while on the run.

"I used to."

"See? You're in the process of switching sides."

"Maybe I secretly like the crispiness of waffles. The fuss and effort that goes into them."

"You like being fussed over?"

"No, not really."

He nodded as though her answer confirmed something. She hoped he didn't think she didn't enjoy flowers and a bit of pampering from time to time.

She continued, "The careful measuring instead of just slapping the batter on a hot pan and knowing it'll form a circle."

"And you're into homemade mix, batter, I'll bet," he said. "Nothing the easy way."

She laughed.

In the swing beside her, Xavier made a foul-sounding noise that suggested he was in need of a fresh diaper, and quite likely a new outfit, as well. A quick check told her she was correct, and she closed her eyes for a second, hoping for serenity and good luck, since this messy diaper was going to mean laundry for Xavier's outfit and the swing seat cover, a bath for him, and maybe one for herself, too.

"I'll run the water," Zach said, moving behind her as she still stood over Xavier in his swing, contemplating where to start.

Since Zach was getting the kitchen sink ready for Xavier's bath, she chose to strip her son down on a receiving blanket there on the floor. Zach was waiting, hands outstretched, ready to take the naked one to the sink.

Catherine bundled the whole mess of clothes, seat cover and blanket into a ball, then headed to the washing machine in the basement while Zach lifted Xavier into the water. As she started the wash cycle, she could hear Zach singing to her son in a low voice.

She slipped up the stairs, curious what song he'd chosen. Xavier was gurgling happily, possibly trying to sing along to what sounded an awful lot like the Sammy Davis Jr. song *I've Gotta Be Me*.

"I didn't know you liked the Rat Pack," she said, entering the kitchen. Zach looked so natural with Xavier, her little boy watching him with big, trusting eyes. It melted her heart. She wanted this man, this connection for her son.

"Their songs were some of my grandma's favorites."

"So you're not actually a soft-hearted romantic,"

she said, as she took the offered baby, who was clean and as slippery as an eel, and wrapped him in a towel. "It's your grandmother's fault that you choose to sing these grand classics?"

"Pretty much."

"Hmm." She gave him what she hoped was a saucy look. He'd been singing with heart. He liked the song and he couldn't hide it—not from her.

Xavier was sleepy and she put him down for a nap, then returned to the kitchen, where Zach was sitting with a cup of coffee. The front of his thin knitted top was still wet from the bathwater, she noted.

"Do you think they'll actually have a reception for us in a week and a half? Or were those ladies just bluffing at the surprise party?" she asked, pouring herself a mug.

She'd grown more and more apprehensive about her ability to brush off the event in the short time frame without inadvertently snubbing people and hurting feelings. Add in the way Zach had clammed up when she'd said yes to the idea, and the event had the potential to really mess things up. And not just because everyone thought it was odd that she didn't want her picture taken. Zach, at least, had seemed to accept her partial truth about being stalked.

"Won't the caffeine keep Xavier up?" Zach asked, as she joined him with her cup of joe.

"If I have more than half a cup, yes."

"Delicate balance."

"I like the taste. As well as living on the edge. So?" she prompted.

"Why not drink decaf?"

She made a face that caused him to laugh.

"And yes," he said, "I think they will do their best to have a reception, as well as the shower for you and I as well as Xavier."

Catherine quieted the worries swimming through her mind. The questions. The thoughts. The doubts.

"Do you want them?" she asked. May as well start at the beginning.

He was watching her, his surprise evident. She'd noticed since yesterday's party that one of his walls, at least, had swung open like the shutter on a window. He no longer tried to hide his emotions. Not all of them. He allowed himself more expression around her, and she realized how closed off and careful he'd been up until now. "Do *you*?" he countered.

"I asked first."

"So? I asked second."

"It doesn't work that way."

"Says who?" He was glowering, but in a playful way, she realized with a skip of her heart.

"Says me," she retorted, with a gentle firmness that she hoped would keep the banter going.

"And you're my wife so your word takes precedence?"

"You're a fast learner." She smiled at him over the rim of her cup. "I like that."

"That was a question, not a declaration," he grumbled, but she noted the twinkle in his eye as he lifted his own coffee.

"So are we having a reception or not?"

"Why should we?" he asked.

For a split second she thought he was giving her a surly retort, but quickly realized he was actually asking, wanting to hash this out with her like a real partner.

"The town expects one."

"And?"

"And they really seem to want one."

"We've covered that already," he said.

"'Want' and 'expect' are two different things."

He tipped his head, ceding her the point. "I suppose."

"I'm afraid that if we, two people with the most unorthodox marriage in town, say no, they will…" She inhaled loudly as she thought through all the possible consequences.

"It's not the most unorthodox."

"Sorry?"

"It's not. Blueberry Springs has gone nuts with marriages of convenience and the like over the past year or two. Although we are the first to do the mail order thing."

"You make it sound like I was shipped in a box."

"Some assembly required."

"For our marriage or for me?" she challenged.

"Your pick." He added, "Don't worry about me and the town. If you start doing things for them and their sake they'll never let you stop."

"Who says I'd be doing it for them?"

"I can see it in your gaze."

"Can not."

"Can so." Zach leaned across the table, his eyes soft and unthreatening. She wasn't uncomfortable with his probing, even though she knew he was looking deep.

For once, she didn't want to hide.

"You're a pleaser," he announced.

"Am not."

"Except with your husband. You're happy enough arguing with him all day long."

She gave him a dark look and huffed, hoping to hide the fact that she wanted to smile.

CATHERINE WAS LETTING Zach stare her down, see that she had doubts about denying the town a baby and bridal shower as well as a reception in their honor. She cared what they thought. Not just for her sake, but for his. He could see it. The hesitation, the worry.

And no, he couldn't kid himself that it was about creating that perfect family and community upbringing for Xavier. She wanted that, but he could tell that a reception and shower weren't about Xavier in her mind. They would be about and for him—Zach. She would pretend their marriage was genuine, that she was his real wife in all ways expected in order for him to keep face around town. She would fake whatever was needed so he wasn't judged.

She was a good woman.

A good woman with a past that sometimes frightened her.

And he didn't have a dossier on her. He didn't have the information he needed so he could do everything in his power to keep her safe. Because that's what he was going to do. Start watching her more closely. Digging for information, in ways that didn't cause her to run.

How was he going to do that?

How was he going to be the man she was beginning to trust, and act like an agent, too?

He shook off his thoughts. He needed to give her a chance to open up on her own. They'd made good progress over the past two days, and if he wasn't careful, he could mess up everything. And then he wouldn't be able to help her.

Patience.

He needed patience.

He felt as though untangling his grandmother's embroidery threads would be easier than this.

He focused back on the conversation, and stated, "You worry that the town will start talking about me and what kind of marriage I got myself into if we don't play it up and celebrate like a real couple?"

She was turning her cup in her hands. It was a fun one from Wally's that said Running Wild in Blueberry Springs, and had a stick figure running from a bear. Rumor was that Jen Kulak had designed it along with some T-shirts.

Catherine stopped fiddling with her mug, her somber eyes meeting his. "Yes."

"And?"

"Do you like to bring in strays who take advantage of you?"

"Sorry?" He had a pretty good idea what she was getting at, but he wanted her to voice it, try and defend the faulty notion, and then kill the very thought where it stood when she realized how ridiculous it all was.

Because in his eyes, it simply wasn't true. She wasn't a stray and their marriage wasn't a pity deed. For either of them.

"Zach, I think you know what I mean." She stood, taking her mug with her, the warm tone she'd been using replaced by a clipped, cool British one.

He hooked his fingers around her wrist, holding her loosely so she wouldn't flee. "Please, explain."

"There's nothing to explain. You're a great guy who everyone respects. There's no love in this marriage and it looks like I'm taking advantage of you. That I'm using you."

Zach released her, the words striking surprisingly deep. "That's not true."

"Which part?"

"People won't think those things."

"They already are—I overheard them at the party."

He reached for her hand again, slipping his fingers through hers, locking her hand gently in his. "Let's vow to not care what others think, and keep this marriage about what really matters. Let's keep it about what works for us, about what we want and need it to be. That's the only way we're going to be happy."

She nodded, her eyes on his hand. He gave a squeeze, and felt the warmth from her reciprocal response travel all the way up his arm and settle in his chest.

She leaned forward, her voice lowering conspiratorially. "So how are we going to wiggle our way out of a shower and reception?"

And in that moment Zach thought Catherine might just be a match for him in ways he hadn't dared hope.

7

*C*atherine had spent days poring over the financial records for Logan and Zach, hoping they were much better with security system installation details than they were with their finances. She considered herself lucky any time she saw a billable number of hours on a scrap of paper, along with a name and the type of system installed.

But by week's end she had a method to determine their flat rate and add-ons, which had resulted in a nice stack of payment-due notices ready to go out in the mail. It was gratifying to be able to pull her weight and help out.

By a stroke of luck, the ladies weren't able to hold the reception right away, earning her and Zach more wiggle room for finding a way out of having one at all. Something about the lady who made the sandwiches being double booked. Catherine would gladly take the delay, although there was still the small issue of the baby-and-bridal shower, which was coming up faster than she was prepared for. Although a shower felt so much easier to handle than a reception.

Realizing there was no more catching up to do with the finances, Catherine sat back in the kitchen chair she'd dragged into a corner of Zach's new basement office. She'd scrounged an old unwanted table from George next door, and along with the new laptop Zach had ordered for her, she had a workstation.

Yesterday, without being asked, Zach had come back from delivering Gran's resized ring, with a stack of fresh file folders and a filing cabinet. He was a thoughtful man and a thoughtful boss. Patient and willing to laugh at himself, and always generous with his customers by erring in their favor.

But most of all, nothing was off-limits, like it had been at the nightclub, when she'd requested certain financials in hopes of having a broader sense of the company and her role in its success. Zach didn't seem to have anything to hide, and despite her being on the lookout, nothing had struck her as odd or sketchy, other than their large pile of unsent invoices. Were they secretly wealthy, so they could afford to be lax about receiving payment for their services? Or was their income coming from other places? Both Zach and Logan were retired from the military, but having a great pension at their age was unlikely.

She'd missed spotting money laundering that had been happening practically under her nose at the nightclub. Was she missing something here, too?

She'd been naïve, though, so certain that the rest of the world wasn't like her family and that what was happening at the club was normal that she'd turned a blind eye to the small signs. The quiet conversations that stopped when she came along. The strangers coming and going from the back room as if they owned the place. The careful redirection whenever she wanted to know more about the financial aspects of the business.

Catherine sat forward and pressed her hands against her lower back, arching and leaning from side to side, stretching her tired muscles. Xavier was getting to the point where he would nap for several hours, giving her plenty of time to dive into her work, but she often forgot to look up and take a break until he awoke.

It had been snowing all week, a storm having moved in, determined to bury the town in white. She had never seen anything like it, and tried not to panic at the way the small window above her workstation was blocked by a pile of snow, and how Zach had had to shovel a foot or two of the fluffy stuff away from their front door that morning so he could go out and clear the sidewalk.

Like anyone would be out walking or even driving in that stuff.

Well, she'd been wrong.

The street had been alive with the sound of snowblowers, calls of hello as the neighbors shoveled their drives, then helped each other finish theirs, as well. Shortly afterward, people had been out walking like it wasn't some sort of snowy version of Armageddon out there.

Through the baby monitor, she heard Xavier starting to gurgle and coo, in his bed beside hers. Picking up the device, Catherine headed up the stairs. In the hall that led to the living room, she met Zach, who was carting an office chair.

"What's that?"

"I got you a chair with lumbar support and armrests."

She couldn't help but smile. The chair was gorgeous and looked very comfortable. She wanted to worry about Zach spending money on things for his business, but seeing how much was owed to him and Logan, a proper chair might be nice.

"The kitchen chair is fine," she said, wanting to assure him she didn't expect to be pampered.

"What if we have company?"

"We can carry it upstairs, silly." She gave a little laugh. She'd learned that when Zach decided something was needed, he made sure it materialized, and there was no use fighting it. She figured a new desk was most likely to appear next, but wanted him to know she didn't expect it. "I've seen your financials. Saving a little money wouldn't be a bad idea." The man spent like money was water coming over the falls.

"I've got savings, and you need a proper chair."

"I'm only sitting for a few hours at a time. I'm all caught up, by the way." She hoped that the sudden, prompt billing shortly after her arrival didn't lead the townspeople to believe she was a money-grubber.

Zach moved past her. "You could still use a proper chair." As he angled his way through the doorway to the basement steps, he called, "I have no interest in being sued because I failed to provide suitable, ergonomic office equipment."

"You can't sue your husband." She thought for a moment. "Can you?"

"Don't get any ideas about finding loopholes."

Shaking her head in amusement, she went to

retrieve Xavier. He kicked his feet when he saw her, filling her heart.

"Hey, my little man. How was your nap?" She kissed his soft cheeks, loving the way they were so doughy and warm, giving in to the light pressure of her lips. Such unconditional, uncomplicated love.

She changed Xavier's diaper, marveling at how much he'd filled out over the past week. His cheeks seemed chubbier, his short legs sporting an extra roll.

"Look at you, getting so big."

His diaper had leaked a bit while he'd slept and she changed him into a borrowed one-piece outfit that had a hippo on the front, the navy blue bringing out the darkness of his eyes and hair.

"Mummy needs to go to the store so she can touch up her roots and look pretty." She gave Xavier kisses all over his belly. Gaining weight and dying her hair had given her a decent all-new identity, one she intended to hold on to. "But it's scary outside. Too much snow for Mum."

She carried Xavier down to the living room, where Zach was wrestling with the chair's large shipping box, snipping the tape so the carton would lie flat. "I suppose Xavier's still too small to enjoy in a cardboard box fort?"

"A little bit. But I'm not."

"Sorry, you missed playtime, Mama."

"When is this snow ever going to end?" she asked, standing in front of the window. She was embarrassed by the amount of dark roots that were showing, and had resorted to a ponytail, hoping Zach hadn't noticed just how far from being a true blonde she actually was.

Outside, the whole street was a winter wonderland of softened shapes and dampened sounds, the pure white coverlet sparkling when the sun made a random appearance. But the storm had also left her housebound, as she didn't know how to drive in these conditions, and the stroller was impossible to push.

She'd seen a mom go by with a set of twins bundled on a sled, marching up and down the street, getting her exercise, while walking the dog, as well.

The problem was, if Catherine asked for a sled Zach would get one. It would be too easy to take advantage of his generosity. Especially since he seemed to enjoy spoiling Xavier. He'd bought the boy a lovely stuffed giraffe and a hippo. Xavier was too young to play with them, but during his tummy time on the rug he loved to stare at the giraffe with his big, beautiful eyes.

Zach came over to stand beside her and watch the falling snow. "It's peaceful."

"Mesmerizing."

He turned away, saying casually, "It will probably end about in April."

"April!" she exclaimed, startling Xavier, who was cozied up against her chest. Catching Zach's expression, she relaxed. "You can't joke about things like that. It's still only November and not officially winter yet! I can't imagine it getting worse than this."

"It's not uncommon to get snow into May around here."

"Zach!"

He flinched, pretending to cower. "What? The mountains and altitude bring on storms and strange weather patterns. It's not my fault."

"I'm blaming you if it snows in May."

"You've got cabin fever?" he asked, becoming a bit more serious.

"I feel like I'm going to go bonkers."

"Then let's go out," he said simply.

"In this?" She could barely see across the street, snowflakes were falling so steadily. It was like the frozen equivalent of a typical rainy November in the UK.

"In this." Zach grinned and headed to the coat closet in the entryway. Seconds later he reappeared with an armload of clothing.

"I don't think I could manage to walk in this. Not with the stroller." She was afraid to use the baby carrier that kept Xavier snug to her chest in case he suffocated under all the layers.

"We're driving." Zach jingled his keys and Catherine's heart lifted, until she sized up the pile of clothing. It was so much work to get ready. But Zach had explained to her the other day, as he'd gotten bundled up to drive to the store for milk—in his repaired Land Rover, which looked amply suited for the weather conditions, as well as a family of three—that you always wanted to be dressed for the worst. He'd listed possible things that would leave you stranded, such as accidents, an icy patch that put you into the ditch, a weather-induced breakdown, or a road closure or avalanche. She hadn't even thought of avalanches being a danger, and now cast a suspicious glance at every peak that dared show itself through the hovering clouds.

"Can we stop at the chemist?" she asked, hoping they carried her usual brand of hair dye so she wouldn't have to puzzle through which brand would be the closest match to her existing color.

"The drugstore? Sure."

"Then I'm in." Taking Xavier's snowsuit so she could begin the process of wrangling him into it, she asked, "Remind me again why I moved here?"

"Because it happens to be where the best men are."

Quite simply, she had to agree.

Having already stopped by the drugstore, Zach led Catherine to the entrance of Brew Babies. The pub held pretty much all the town's nightlife under one roof. While it didn't open for another few hours, he knew Moe was expecting him, as Zach and Ethan had been working together to update his wiring and technology in hopes of increasing his internet speed.

Zach carried Xavier in the car seat, Catherine having grown comfortable with him taking the boy more and more often, even allowing him to scoop Xavier up if he was fussing while she showered in the mornings. Progress. Same with how the smudges under her eyes had disappeared, replaced with a healthy glow that made her look a little bit like that actress from *Titanic*. British, flushed and lively, blonde and curvy, and pretty much his ideal woman when it came to looks. That Catherine didn't take him too seriously was simply icing on the already delicious cake. He was a lucky man.

He hurried to reach the door first, crunching across the snow. He swung it open for his bride and she stepped in, stomping the snow off her boots. They paused for a moment to allow their eyes to become accustomed to the dimmer light inside.

"We aren't allowed to serve babies," Moe said. He came around the long counter at the other end of the pub, where he'd been unpacking a box of new wineglasses.

"Babies is in your name, and doesn't most of what you serve come out of bottles?" Zach quipped.

"Funny. I'll have to try that one on Amy."

"Did I hear my name?" Amy came down the hall where the office and washrooms were, massaging her lower back. She was about five months pregnant and, as far as Zach could tell, as happy as could be. The kind of happy most people longed for. He might even be hoping for a little bit of it himself.

"You must be Catherine," she said. "I'm so sorry I missed meeting you at the surprise party. Since we bought the pub a few months ago, it's been a little bit crazy keeping up with it all." Amy came forward and gave Catherine a welcoming hug, which seemed to take his wife by surprise. "Ginger McGinty is beside herself over how Zach found himself someone without her. Be sure to rub that in whenever you can." She smiled and bent to look at Xavier, so Zach hoisted the carrier and sleeping boy higher. "Oh, he is even more adorable than everyone's been saying."

"You must be about five or six months along?" Catherine asked.

Amy beamed and nodded. "Five and a half."

"You may as well come in," Moe said, as they were all still standing near the doors. "I doubt we'll get fined for having a minor in here, since we're technically closed and not serving alcohol."

"I always forget your pubs aren't like the UK's," Catherine said, taking in the establishment. "Ours allow minors."

Zach moved to the bar and slid onto a stool, then placed the car seat on the counter. He adjusted the carrier, making sure it was safe where it was, and then unzipped the snowsuit Xavier was bundled up in, so he wouldn't grow too warm.

"This is nice, though," Catherine said, taking in the quiet room. A few tables, a jukebox, the long bar and a temporary stage pretty much made up the place.

Zach caught Amy and Moe sharing a proud look.

"It's like a nightclub and pub mixed together." Catherine was rubbing her crossed arms like she was cold, but Zach wondered if it was something else. Something about being in the bar.

"Can I get you anything?" Moe asked. "The

kitchen is still closed and I can't serve alcohol, but soda or a water?"

"Water would be lovely, thanks," Catherine said, after which Zach offered Moe the two separate price quotes Catherine had whipped up on the computer.

She already had an amazing system, with nicely labeled folders, and it made him wonder how they'd gotten by without her.

Well, they hadn't really. Which explained why his savings had dipped so low and how his pension felt like it shrank every month. At least now money would be coming in reliably, covering their costs and more.

He couldn't believe he and Logan had let it ride for so long. They were lucky to still be in business.

"Catherine did up two options for you." He smiled at the pride he heard in his own voice. Dang, but wasn't he a lucky man? Had he already thought that today? How about this hour? Because he was. Truly was.

Moe pulled the sheet toward him and gave it a glance, elbows resting on the bar's surface. "Which would you recommend?"

Zach spun the sheet so he could read the bottom number. The price difference was negligible, but he knew Moe and Amy were being careful with their money, seeing as they had a baby on the way. Something Zach understood. Having Xavier in the house had changed a few of his financial priorities, too, and oddly enough, he no longer seemed to find the urge to max out his credit card during late-night online shopping sprees. Although he had developed an inexplicable urge to buy the kid everything he could possibly want.

He needed to be wise with his money, as Catherine had suggested. It wasn't just him now. He couldn't simply list the house if times got tight, and take some high-paying, dangerous job to fill his bank account again.

"Option two makes it easier to expand your network later down the line, and will allow for heavier streaming," Zach said. "However, unless Blueberry Springs suddenly improves their infrastructure, you're not that likely to find yourself needing that in the next few years. Plus, you can always come back and expand what you set up with option one."

They discussed a few more details while Catherine and Amy chatted about babies and pregnancy.

Decision made, Moe filled in Amy, who agreed with his choice.

Moe turned to Catherine. "I heard you're doing the books for Zach and Logan."

"I am," she said.

"She's doing a great job," Zach stated, even though it wasn't necessary.

"Are you looking for more work?" Moe asked. "We could use some help keeping the bar's accounts straight and on track. Just a few hours here and there."

Catherine opened her mouth and glanced around the pub, her mind obviously whirling. Zach didn't know much about her past, but the dark look that shadowed her gaze told him before she said so that despite this being a decent job working for good people, her answer was going to be no.

CATHERINE HAD HESITATED for a few beats too long. She could feel the way Zach had noted that, tucking the fact away to use as a hint to try to crack into her past. He was like that. Silently aware. All the time.

She loved it.

Except for when she didn't.

"I could use more work," she said carefully. "However, I don't think I'm equipped to do the books for something as large as a nightclub." Had her voice tightened when she'd said the word *nightclub*? She didn't think so, but her throat had definitely seized up a little. "But thank you for thinking of me."

"You sure?" Moe asked. "The job's yours—as much of it as you want." Beside him, Amy nodded.

"That's very kind."

"It's not beyond your reach," Zach said. His voice was soft, coaxing.

Confidence wasn't the issue. In fact, she was quite confident. Confident she could not work in another nightclub, even if it seemed warm, cozy and friendly.

"No, thank you," she said, wincing at the sharpness of her reply. "I'm not ready for something like this." And she wasn't. She was scared she'd land herself in the same old predicament as last time.

"We could send you to the city for training," Zach offered. Moe and Amy shared a small shrug, wordlessly agreeing.

"And what would I do with Xavier?" She fussed with one of his booties. "The whole idea is for me to be able to work around his schedule."

Moe and Amy had eased away, no doubt aware that this was quickly becoming a fight. Their first fight as a couple.

Were they a couple?

As flatmates, then? Because they were not a couple. There wasn't even any attraction there. Other than the purely physical kind, which counted for nothing but a boatload of trouble. And the banter and jokes they had? Good friends had that. Flatmates, too.

"You're right. It's too much," Zach said casually, sending Catherine mentally off balance. He was pulling back from the verbal tussle as if he'd already been knocked out.

She turned away, unsure how to react to what had felt like an unintended dig.

So was that it? Fight over? What was his long game?

As she pondered their fight, a cowboy came in and sat down at the other end of the bar. He was wearing a hat and boots, and looked like he may have ridden up on a horse.

"Can I get a whiskey yet?" he asked Moe.

"Nope," he replied.

"Aw, man," muttered the cowboy. "We're still before hours?"

"We are, Cole."

The man spun away from the bar, pausing as though debating whether to stick it out until opening or not. He spotted Catherine and winked.

She turned back to Zach and Xavier.

At least it looked as though Moe was a stickler when it came to obeying local serving laws. Catherine liked that. But just because he didn't serve outside the permitted hours didn't mean he wouldn't shift money around under the table or avoid paying his taxes.

"And doing the accounting here isn't 'too much' for me to handle if I wanted to," Catherine said to Zach, unable to resist taking up the argument again.

"Okay."

"Okay." She sat a little straighter, her eyes locked on the bottles of liquor lined up against a mirror on the opposite wall. Her gaze was resolute, her cheeks hot. She caught Zach's eye and this time refused to be the first to look away.

"It's not too much for you," he repeated simply, opening his clasped hands.

"It's not!" She spun to face him instead of his reflection.

"Okay." He wasn't nearly as insistent as she was, and it was making her flustered. He'd thrown her off and gotten under her skin.

"Can you guys help us out over here when you've finished your lovers' spat?" Moe called.

Zach tipped his chin upward, acknowledging Moe. He said to Catherine, "So we agree that it's not too much."

He calmly slid off his stool, hand extended to help Catherine off her own. She refused his assistance.

"It's not too much at all," she said, tossing her

ponytail behind her as she flounced toward the makeshift stage over by the jukebox.

She heard Zach mutter, "I do love a sassy woman."

She fought the urge to turn and stick out her tongue. Knowing Zach, he might take it as an invitation to do something that would make her body throb and her head grow light.

Wait...if they were in agreement...had she just inadvertently agreed to something? Such as the nightclub's accounting? He'd turned that whole argument around on her. She put her hands on her hips and spun to face Zach, causing him to bump into her. His hands slipped around her waist, bracing her against him. He felt good. Too good.

"You don't get to mess with my mind, you hear me?"

"I do."

"Which is it? You do get to mess with my mind, or you do hear me?"

He was watching her with a sincere, forthright gaze that made her anger dissolve. He didn't know why she feared working the books here in the bar; he only saw what she'd done to fix his. He believed in her. Didn't understand her, but was cool about it all just the same. It made her want to roll up onto her tiptoes and kiss him.

Oh, she was a mess, wasn't she? She turned to

Moe and Amy, disentangling herself from Zach. "What do you need?" she asked.

"We want to test the karaoke system."

"Lovely." Catherine stepped to the stage and took the microphone.

"That's not too much?" Zach teased. "To sing?"

She glowered at him, silently telling him to watch it. "How about a duet?" she asked sweetly, a challenge weighting her words.

"Would love to." Zach hopped onto the stage with ease. "Got a second microphone?"

Moe shook his head. "One thing at a time, pal."

Cole spoke up, pushing back his cowboy hat. "That gal at the town office…"

"Nicola?" Moe suggested.

"Yeah, that's the one. She said the second microphone will be here in time for tomorrow night's turkey sing-off, or whatever she called it."

"She comes up with the best ideas," Amy said, her head bent as she adjusted a few knobs on the sound system. "I wish she was still working full-time."

"If this is a turkey sing-off, does that mean we're the turkeys?" Catherine asked Zach. "Because if so, I'm going to win. It's a Team Waffles thing."

"You brought me up here, Pancake."

"Not a pancake. I'm a waffle."

"I thought you were a turkey."

"You could have said no to the challenge." She gave him a slow scan from his toes to his nose, implying that if he'd done so he'd be lacking as a man.

"I could have."

"But you didn't."

"Maybe I'm not all that smart."

"Best singer wins a turkey for Thanksgiving dinner," called Cole. He had that perfect twang you heard in the movies.

"A live one?" Catherine asked. "Heaven help me, please say no."

"No."

She pretended to wipe sweat from her brow. Although, if Zach continued to stand so close, she might just start sweating. There was something about having him so near that made her very aware of how manly he was from the heat radiating off him to the way his aftershave smelled.

"Can you sing?" she asked.

"I'll make you swoon."

"Pick a song, Mr. Confident."

"And you'll sing it?"

"And so will you. Duet, remember?"

Zach jumped off the stage, making his way to the laptop Moe was fiddling with.

"Catherine, is your mic on?" Moe asked.

"Testing, testing," she said into it.

Amy gave her a thumbs-up and adjusted a few things.

"We should really do this tomorrow night. What if the settings gets bumped?" Amy said to Moe.

"We won't have time, and we have willing victims ready to sing for us now."

Catherine couldn't help but notice the way the two were always stepping into each other's physical space, casually touching. Like right now Amy was dragging her fingers along the waistband of Moe's jeans, as if wishing for something.

Catherine inhaled and dragged her glance away, catching Zach watching her. If she wasn't careful she'd start wishing for things with her own husband.

"Well?" She stuck out a hip, giving him an impatient look that made him smile.

"How do you do with the oldies?" he asked.

"Try me, Grandma's boy."

He smirked as the first chords of the song began to play. Moe tapped a button, then crossed his arms to lean back and listen.

Catherine knew the song, "Baby, It's Cold Outside," and she lifted the microphone closer to her lips, mentally running through the lyrics so she'd be ready for her turn to sing.

"The best version was sung by Johnny Mercer

155

and Margaret Whiting," she said, loudly enough for Zach to hear.

"Agreed. But Dean Martin is known best for making the song famous and melting hearts."

"The song isn't about implied nonconsent," she added, noting how in recent years it had gotten a bad rap due to the way the man tries hard to be convincing in regards to making his sweetheart stay with him a little longer despite the night growing older.

"It's about resisting temptation." Zach met her eyes with a heated look that nearly turned her into a puddle right then and there.

She almost missed her first line, wondering if she'd be able to resist the temptation that was Zach, or if she'd end up like the woman in the song, saying to heck with what everyone thought about her and giving in to her wants.

She sang her line, her voice a bit rusty as it had been a long time since she'd felt the urge to sing in a heartfelt way. Zach, leaning in to share the microphone, delivered his line flawlessly, his timing perfect, his words flowing into hers and vice versa as they got into the groove of the duet and the overlapping lines. He had a rich voice—that same one he'd used to sing to Xavier. But now it was throatier somehow. Deeper. It felt like he was singing to her and only her.

Which was ridiculous.

He was singing *with* her. It just felt like he was singing to her because he kept looking at her. Probably because he was afraid they'd knock heads while sharing the microphone if he didn't know where she was at all times.

Her voice came back as she relaxed, enjoying the timing that came so easily between her and Zach. Her husband.

"Why am I not surprised he chose an old song?" Moe asked Amy. She was smiling, swaying to the music, and Moe took her in his arms, dancing and making Catherine smile.

"Not bad for something that's not country and western," the cowboy said.

Catherine faced Zach, the push-pull arguments of the female and male vocals feeling as though it was mirroring her own life with Zach. The two singers argued back and forth over the pros and cons of the woman staying for another drink and allowing things to go a little bit further. The couple in the song was playing a coy game, the tension and desire building between them, echoing the situation between herself and Zach.

Catherine's own lyrics were about avoiding judgment, reminding her of her own experience. The judgment she'd faced due to her family's reputation. Then from them as she chose to live her life separately. From the police when she'd been taken in. From strangers when they discovered she was a single mother. The wary watching of the folks here in Blueberry Springs, generous as they were, yet ensuring she took care of Zach.

But most of all, for saying yes. For taking the leap and marrying Zach, when society said no, that's not what you do.

Why had Zach chosen this song?

He was swaying beside her, flirtatious and debonair, like a lover who was trying to be convincing. Like a man trying to convince a woman to stay for another drink. To cozy up by the fire. He waggled his brows and she let out a surprised laugh. He smiled and ran a light finger between her brows, where tension always formed, and pretended to wipe it away. He must have noticed her falling in on herself, thinking about her life and becoming tense.

She shifted her body away, then back again, acting coy, playing the game. She forgot everything but him as they sang the final chorus together, their voices melding in perfect harmony.

If this was life with Zach, she never wanted the song to end.

8

*Z*ach felt alive. Really, truly alive. Like he'd just lived a whole entire life in one short song. A song he'd chosen in order to toy with his wife, but which had opened up his world. He couldn't explain it, but didn't want the feeling to end. He wanted to keep singing.

"You were awesome," he said. "What if we'd never discovered we could do that?"

She leaned against him, her hand on his chest. "*We* were awesome." She was looking up at him, her expression open, free. She was beautiful.

Without thinking, he leaned down, matching his lips to hers.

He kissed her.

Pulled back.

Said nothing.

Didn't tug her into his arms.

Didn't inhale the scent of her perfume, her shampoo.

"Oh," Catherine said, taking a half step back, looking shy and flustered.

Zach stepped off the stage. He didn't know what to do with her surprise, only knew that he had to walk away or he'd pull her into his arms and give her a long, deep kiss that would claim her.

A woman he wasn't allowed to claim, because she hadn't given him the word. She had to let those walls down on her own. He wasn't going to be like the man in the song and push his luck. She had to let him in. On her terms. In her time.

But he really hoped she would hurry it up.

"That was amazing," Amy gushed. She was holding her phone, and Zach had a feeling she'd recorded them, the two of them too wrapped up in the spell they'd created to even notice the pub owners working on the system around them. The speakers had changed location from when the song had started and he hadn't noticed. It was a good thing he hadn't married Catherine while he was still in the spy business or on his first mission he would have likely been hit by a car while crossing the street.

"You two should take it on the road," Cole said, tipping his cowboy hat.

"Thanks." Zach turned to Amy. "Don't post that video online, okay?"

"Why?"

"Please."

"Okay," Amy said, looking disappointed.

Catherine was still onstage, still looking a little shell-shocked. That had to be good, right?

"Maybe you could be the karaoke night's opening act," Zach called to her.

"The best karaoke places seed the crowd with a few semiprofessionals," Catherine replied. Her voice had sort of a dazed tone.

"Really?" Amy asked.

She nodded. "We used to do that at the night-club I—" She sucked in a breath, her eyes darting to the left. "—went to." She flapped her hands nervously and came down off the stage. "I used to be a clubber."

"Clubber of what? Of baby seals?" Cole asked with a wry laugh. He turned to Moe. "Could really use that whiskey."

"We're not open."

"I think she means nightclub," Zach said, knowing Cole was being smart.

"A lifetime ago," Catherine said stiffly. "I'm a mum now." She had a hint of that proper British thing going on as she moved toward the still-sleeping Xavier on legs that could have been metal rods, for all the flex and bounce they had. She took her old stool, and Zach sat beside her, curious about the change in her.

She'd been shocked by the kiss.

But this stiffness? This was about the nightclub back home.

So what had gone down on the other side of the world? Was the club related to her stalker? Zach would bet he had the correct answer on that one: yes.

He was sorely tempted to give Logan the go-ahead on snooping into her past. Because now that he'd had a taste of her lips, of the way the two of them could move and sing together up on stage, he didn't want a single thing to get in the way of having this dream become reality.

CATHERINE NEEDED TO CONTROL HERSELF. She'd gotten swept up in the moment and the connection she'd felt with Zach. A man she was afraid to trust, even though she knew it was already too late. She trusted him. And because she did, she was allowing things she wanted to keep secret to tumble from her lips.

And the kiss…

He'd kissed her sweetly and without expectations.

A kiss that held promise.

A kiss that had been an offer. A key slipped under her door, welcoming her to unlock the heat simmering between them, following the duet. It had been undeniable, the sense of potential, excitement and freedom ripping through her, shredding anything that stood in her way of having this man.

She'd momentarily forgotten who she was. A gang leader's daughter. The little girl who'd been scoffed at for wanting to do things the honest way. The young woman whose brothers had beaten up her first lover for taking her offered virginity.

With that small slip about the club, she'd almost told Zach who she really was. He wasn't dumb, and she knew that once he pieced enough tidbits together and saw what she'd left behind and why, things would change. The discomfort would slide in like a ghost, wedging its way between them. There'd be extra glances, to check in on her and to confirm her real intentions. There'd be loaded statements, jokes that weren't funny. A subtle uptick in looking over his shoulder, as though expecting someone from her family to be there.

Zach was too quick and too smart not to notice and add it all up.

What would his clients think about having someone from a crime family doing his books and sending out invoices? It didn't matter that she was honest. Her family's history and reputation would taint her, paint her with the same brush as though she was truly one of them. The changes would be subtle. Clients double-checking to ensure her billing was accurate. A downturn in his company acquiring new accounts. An increase in questions about the integrity of a system he'd installed and who could disarm it.

Zach shifted on the bar stool beside her. "You worked in a pub?" he asked.

She turned slowly, afraid what she'd see in her husband's eyes. Those beautiful blue eyes that were always watching.

She'd lied to him, and that wasn't who she wanted to be. But most importantly, not who she wanted him to think she was.

She was caught, though. How could she protect herself as well as Xavier if she told the truth?

"Nightclub," she said, keeping her voice low enough that Amy and Moe couldn't hear them from their spot at the end of the bar. They were looking at a booklet of available song titles, each page flip punctuated by laughter. Cole was sitting nearby, hands clasped on the countertop, contemplating his thumbnail, and too far away from Catherine and Zach to eavesdrop.

"What went wrong?" Zach asked.

She noted that he hadn't asked what had happened, or whether she'd liked the job.

"What didn't?" She tried for a chuckle to ease the tightness in her chest, but ended up choking instead.

"You want to talk about it?" he asked, when she'd ceased coughing.

"Not especially."

They sat in silence for a moment. Zach was pointedly not looking at her, giving her space, idly rocking Xavier in his carrier. It was tempting to tell him everything.

"But you should know," she said quietly. She liked Zach and she wanted this—whatever it was—to work. And to do that, she needed to be as upfront and honest as possible. If she started lying now it wouldn't stop until the truth surfaced in one awful tangled mess. And she knew exactly where dishonesty and large omissions led when it came to relationships.

Zach had stilled, his shoulders tipping toward her as he waited and listened.

Her heart was racing like she was being chased as she fought for the courage to let Zach in—just a little bit. Enough that what they had could be based on honesty.

"It closed down," she said, forcing the words

through her tightening throat and past her lips. "I was the events manager for several years. I also did some light accounting and a bit of record keeping and invoicing for the bands I booked."

Her mind swept back through time to the nightclub, the pulse of bass throbbing in her chest while she worked. The flash of strobe lights, the sense of excitement over what each night would bring and whether a celebrity would come by. The place had been trendy, busy even on weeknights, and the profits had made her grin with pride.

Although apparently a substantial amount of those profits hadn't been from her bookings.

"What happened?" Zach asked.

"The club was a cover for a gang." She met his gaze, surprised by the lack of emotion she felt. It was as if someone had numbed her entire nervous system. "They were laundering money."

"Were you brought in by the police?"

She nodded. "But I wasn't—I was in the dark." The sharp sting of humiliation hit her through the numbness. No matter how she lived her life, she felt as though her family would always taint it, and would always find a way to intrude on whatever she managed to set aside for herself.

She could feel Zach's presence beside her, his steady warmth as his gaze took her in, giving her way too much space to voice her secrets.

"I'm sorry, Zach."

"Why?"

"I should have told you sooner. I understand if you no longer want me working with your financials."

"Why?"

"Because…" She waved a hand through the air as though summing up her story. Hadn't he been listening? Why would he want to be associated with someone who had been involved—even unwittingly—with a business that had been closed down due to money laundering charges? "I was associated."

"Did you help launder money?"

"Not intentionally."

"Help assist in tax evasion?"

She leaned back, feeling insulted. "No." Did she look like she would?

"Steal?"

"No!"

"Anything illegal or unethical?"

Catherine fumed at him, then said, "I once gave a friend a drink on the house because it was her birthday."

Zach's chest bounced, his shoulders shaking as he held in a quiet laugh. "And that's got you all strung up tighter than a kitten in a ball of Christmas lights?"

She tugged the hem of her shirt into place and tried not to huff at him.

He draped an arm across her shoulders. "Oh, Catherine." He planted a chaste kiss against her temple, then withdrew, retreating back to his own space. She wanted to follow, wanted to relish his acceptance a little while longer. She wanted to hear him say her name with that hint of affection one more time, and craved to have his lips land against her flesh once again. Only longer next time.

Because this…this was almost too much. Almost like a dream come true.

―――――――

ZACH WAS WELL aware that Catherine hadn't told him the whole truth about the money laundering scheme. He felt as if she'd left some things out, as her sense of responsibility seemed to outweigh the wrongdoing. Embarrassed and ashamed, yes. But to still feel so responsible? That was a good indicator that something wasn't lining up quite right. Whatever it was, he knew it was just another thread in the story of Catherine's past that he'd yet to unravel, like the lengths of yarn tangled at his grandmother's feet.

As Zach guided Catherine to his Land Rover, Xavier dozing in the car seat he was carrying, he said, "You know money laundering is difficult to sniff out. The whole scheme is designed to go undetected."

Catherine took Xavier and focused on securing his carrier in the SUV. Zach watched, forcing himself to consider that she might not be as innocent as his gut suggested.

He took the brush out of the back and began sweeping the accumulated snow off his vehicle. Catherine was in the front seat, seat belt secured, mittened hands clenched in her lap. What would it take to unwind her again? Was he going to have to find a way to get her back on that karaoke stage?

"It must've been a while ago," he said, once he was in the driver's seat.

Yeah, yeah, he was fishing like an agent might, but he told himself he was being supportive. A supportive husband. It was either this or send Logan digging into her past, and that felt like a major breach of trust right now.

"I should have seen the signs."

"Why's that?"

She turned to him, eyes blazing. "Because." She was adamant, but didn't clarify why, simply cinched her seat belt tighter, as if it might help her keep her fears and guilt locked inside.

"I'm a good secret keeper." He gave her a nod and a serious look, playfully pretending to zip up his lips, lock them, then toss the make-believe key over his right shoulder. "See?" he mumbled through closed lips. He opened them to add, "I can't tell anybody anything. My lips are sealed, plus we're under the cone of silence right now. Anything that happens in here will not be heard elsewhere and can never escape."

She didn't reply for a long moment and he gave her a light nudge.

"You seem to be able to speak just fine at the moment despite your so-called locked lips," she said.

"That was for illustration purposes. I'm not a ventriloquist. I find them a little bit creepy, actually."

The hitch that had been tightening her shoulders loosened its grip, and her hands almost unclenched.

"I'm a good listener," he coaxed.

"Is that because of your grandmother?"

"She trained me in many notable ways."

"Fine. You want to know?"

"Yes." He started driving toward home, figuring it would be easier for her to open up if his attention was split between her and the road.

"I can't stand the fact that I aided them unwittingly. People trusted us."

He made a supportive sound, encouraging her to keep talking.

"I thought I was doing a good thing. I brought in good bands and ensured that our club maintained a good reputation. We cared about our patrons and our neighborhood. We had breathalyzers, and free rides home for those in need. We were a responsible nightclub."

He made another supportive sound.

"People *trusted* us. And I thought we were good people, but we weren't." Her hands flew up in the air. "I feel so...so..."

"Betrayed?"

She let out a shaky sigh, her shoulders collapsing. "And taken advantage of."

"At least they weren't off murdering people," he joked. "You know, whacking people in the back room."

Her face collapsed, and he could tell she was wondering if something like that had indeed occurred.

"Typically, that stuff only happens in movies," he said quickly.

She shook her head. "I'm sure it happens, but hopefully it didn't at the club." There was a resignation in her voice, a sorrow he couldn't quite understand.

"It happens here. All over the world." And more

often than the average person realized. Maybe that was the reason for Catherine's distress. She was an average person and it made sense that discovering how she'd been assisting in creating a front to mask illegal activities would weigh heavily on her. "Sometimes people do bad things. All we can do is try and put more good out into the world."

He glanced her way, and found her eyes damp and full of gratitude.

He pulled into the garage a moment later, the dim light filtering in around them.

"I'm glad I found you," she said.

She leaned across the console between them, lightly planting a kiss on his cheek that broke a small piece of him. He wasn't sure what it was, only that it was one he had used to protect himself, to shelter himself from feeling the things that were slowly spilling out in regards to the woman across from him, his wife.

9

*C*atherine wasn't sure what to do. Xavier wouldn't settle and she was so tired she felt like she was quickly becoming a sleep-deprived zombie due to several nights of restlessness. Xavier's sniffles and sneezes, which had caused the ladies to postpone Catherine's baby-and-bridal shower, had swelled into a barking cough. It was startling, so much sound coming from such a small body, and the only thing that seemed to help was to hold him against her shoulder and pace the room.

Was he feverish? How had she not thought to pick up a baby thermometer? She'd thought to get hair dye to touch up her roots, but not a thermometer? What kind of mother was she?

The furnace kicked on and her bedroom grew stuffy and warm. Xavier's coughing seemed to grow worse and she opened the door, stepping into the cool, dark hallway. She continued to pace with him, knowing he was too small for cough medicine, but unsure what she could do to make him comfortable.

Maybe she could use the accounting laptop downstairs and do a quick online search to see if there was reason to worry, or if there was something she could do to help him.

No, she'd just freak herself out, like she had when she'd researched oddities in her pregnancy. Things that had been normal, but that quick searches had made sound fatal.

This was just a cough. A really nasty cough.

He felt so frail, so small and helpless. So vulnerable. How much could a small boy handle?

None of her friends back home were mothers, and she tried to think if she'd overheard women talking about what to do to calm a baby's cough.

She decided it was worth the risk of freaking herself out with an online search, on the off chance she could find something helpful.

Catherine tiptoed past Zach's bedroom, the door of which was closed even though it was only eleven. He'd been out late with Logan a lot lately, the two of them keeping odd hours, often working evenings or even in the middle of the night if someone's security system went off.

Catherine yawned. She'd been in a deep sleep before Xavier's cough had woken her, and now felt dazed and groggy, at the edge of reason, where a sense of sanity and emotional stability were hard to come by.

After heading to the basement, she fired up the laptop, continuing to bounce Xavier on her shoulder.

She sat in her chair, trying to type with one hand while keeping him comforted. He arched his back, nearly tumbling out of her hold. She curved him into the cradle of her left arm and began typing again, but he struggled and squirmed.

She stood, righting him once more. "What's wrong, little buddy? What can your mum do for you?"

Xavier began crying, his cough worsening again. She paced, concerned with how the more he cried, the worse his coughing got.

A light flicked on at the basement stairs and feet padded down the steps.

"I'm sorry if we woke you," Catherine said, when Zach appeared, wearing nothing more than a pair of plaid boxer shorts.

"Sounds like Xavier needs to stop smoking. He's got quite the cough," Zach said casually, seemingly unaffected by the racking sounds coming from her poor son. Zach ran a hand over his bare midsection, and if she hadn't been so distraught, Catherine would have taken a moment to memorize the way he looked, from his tousled hair to his broad shoulders and chest, which tapered down to a slim waist and flat stomach. The man was eye candy.

"I don't know what to do for his cough," she said, her voice trembling. "I wanted to search online, but every time I stop walking his cough gets worse. He's so uncomfortable."

Zach took Xavier, propping the baby upright against his bare chest. "What's got you down, little guy?" He bounced the boy and walked, saying to Catherine, "You can go back to sleep if you want. I can watch him for a while."

"What if there's something wrong with him? Should I take him to a doctor?"

"It sounds like croup."

"Croup? What's that?" Catherine asked. Whatever it was, it didn't sound good.

"Does he have a fever?" Zach asked.

"I don't know."

He touched Xavier's cheek and forehead with the back of his hand. The boy gave a massive cough, struggling to catch enough wind at the end.

"Let's try and open those airways," Zach said to him. The baby let out a small whimper, as though agreeing to his suggestion.

Zach climbed the stairs two at a time, flicking on lights as he went. He tugged a blanket off the living room couch as he passed through to the patio, wrapping it around his shoulders as well as Xavier before pulling on the tall, clunky boots he kept at the patio door. As he stepped into the backyard, a plume of warm air created a cloud around him before he slid the glass door closed.

"You're going to freeze!" Catherine exclaimed from her side of the glass. Xavier wasn't wearing a hat and was sick, so being out in the sub-zero temperature was crazy. And Zach wasn't wearing anything more than underwear and boots. That blanket wasn't going to keep them warm enough.

Zach snugged the blanket around Xavier, rocking back and forth in the weak glow of light coming through the glass. His bare knees stuck out between the bottom of the blanket and the top of his boots.

Catherine fretted, unsure what to do. Taking a sick baby out in the freezing night didn't seem like a smart solution, but Zach had been so confident she hadn't spoken up. Finally, she summoned the courage to go outside and claim her child, certain both males had to be sporting frostbite by now.

She slid the door open and Zach, with a peaceful expression, peeled the blanket away from Xavier's face for a second. The boy's mouth, which had been tight only minutes ago, was slack, his body melting into Zach's.

Catherine lunged forward, worried that Xavier was no longer breathing. But there were little puffs of air forming clouds in front of his face as the cold air nipped closer, his chest moving without labor.

It was a miracle. How was it even possible?

She looked up at Zach, who gave a tender smile. "The cool air helps sooth the swelling in his airways."

"How do you know this?"

"I used to babysit," he said simply. "Sometimes a warm, steamy bathroom helps, too."

Catherine shivered in the cold, not quite ready to go back inside and leave them. Zach held out an arm, his fingers clutching a corner of the blanket as though he was a child making a superhero cape out of bedding. And as Catherine curved under his wing, she thought that maybe he truly was a little bit of a superhero.

ZACH SETTLED Catherine on the couch with the blanket once Xavier's breathing was steady enough that he felt he could safely bring the baby back in-doors. He and Xavier had been sheltered on the porch, the blanket creating a cocoon, so he could watch the stars while the cold air performed a speedy miracle on Xavier's croup. It was one of those indescribable nights where the air was soft and cool, not the typical knifing cold that sank its teeth into your skin as soon as you dared expose any.

Holding the small, warm infant against his chest had felt right even with the cold nipping gingerly at Zach's exposed legs. Snuggling Catherine in their cocoon had felt right, too. She belonged in his arms, and together the three of them made a family.

And when the two of them had begun first humming the Dean Martin song, then outright singing *I've Gotta Be Me* to Xavier, he'd felt as though his heart was going to burst.

Now that Xavier was settled in his swing, still breathing comfortably, Catherine, who had been wound tight with worry, was now sliding down the spiral into exhaustion.

Zach adjusted the blanket, ensuring it was covering her feet, just as she sat up, taking in the sleeping Xavier. "What if his chin drops while he's sleeping and he can't breathe?"

The boy was no longer a newborn, but a three-month-old who was strong enough to move his head around as needed, but Zach understood

179

Catherine's worry, how the croup scare had taken her for a ride.

"Sleeping sitting up will help keep his chest clear," he said, knowing she already knew all this, but needed to hear it again, needed the reassurance. "He'll be more comfortable. And the swing is designed to keep sleeping babies safe."

Catherine eased back into the cushions again, burrowing into their plumpness. But moments later she was swinging her legs over the side of the couch.

"I don't think I should sleep," she said.

"Then we'll both stay up and watch the news." He picked up the remote and turned on the TV, then muted the news station. "That always keeps me awake," he said without humor. All those horrible things going on in the world. He knew that what the reporters had unearthed was only the beginning, topsoil covering the bedrock.

Catherine yawned and Zach figured it wouldn't be long before sleep overtook her, whether she was willing or not.

"Do you want me to get your pillow?" he asked.

"I'm fine."

"You sure? I'll stay up if you want to catch up on your sleep. He's okay now. I've got this."

"Are you certain?" Catherine asked. She was sinking back into the cushions again.

"I'm sure."

She gave a small smile and yawned. "Okay."

"Unless," he said mischievously, "you'd prefer that I tuck you into your bed? I could put the swing in there and we could spoon while watching Xavier sleep."

Her smile widened despite her attempts to rein it in. "While that sounds tempting…"

Zach had moved to sit in the armchair, and glanced up to see if she'd fallen asleep midsentence. Her attention was on the news, her jaw slack, a deep crease between her brows.

He slowly turned to face the television, afraid of what he might see, what kind of memories it might trigger.

It was just the same old type of story he always shut off, this one about the Davies gang over in Britain. He was tired of swallowing how agents came into a situation, did their work, then left, sometimes causing an aftermath that harmed innocent civilians. In this situation, the rumor from Logan was that their acquaintance Whitman, an MI6 agent, had infiltrated the outer ring of the family gang and been responsible for one of the biggest and fastest convictions of organized crime in the history of the UK. Good on him. Unfortunately, a few days after the convictions, their estranged daughter had gone missing, days after her rumored boyfriend, died in a suspicious-sounding car crash. Her death was assumed. A casualty in the name of the greater good.

But Zach couldn't swallow it any longer. He'd seen one photo of her. She'd been a lean, dark-haired, good-looking woman, sporting sunglasses, a floppy sunhat and a giant smile. She was like Catherine—so much potential. So much life in that smile. But while he'd been powerless to help the Davies daughter, he wasn't powerless to help Catherine.

Zach almost looked away from the TV when he caught the story's caption. One of the gang's most lethal members, Jerry Davies, had broken out of jail. How had that happened?

He rubbed his jaw, wondering what the gang had planned. Undoubtedly, there were still a lot of willing associates out on the loose, eager to help a family who, despite being behind bars, likely still wielded a fair amount of power in the crime community.

Remembering Catherine's reaction, he turned to her. She was lying back on the couch, as stiff as a three-day-old corpse. Her eyes were closed and she looked as though she was fighting an internal pain that ran deep.

"You all right?"

She opened her eyes, and flashed a smile so fake

it wouldn't fool a blind person. "Just tired." She closed them again, and Zach went over and tucked the blanket around once more, his concern growing.

Tears formed between her lashes, and she whispered, "That's not the world I want to raise Xavier in."

"You won't," Zach assured her.

He reminded himself that her reaction was normal. That in real life people got upset by the news. They weren't trained to hide it like he and his buddies were. Expressed emotion didn't have to mean anything from an overtired mother. It didn't have to mean that she was hiding something criminal or that she was a woman on the run.

"It's just the media network creating a fuss for ratings. The story's happening a world away," he said gently.

"A world away," Catherine repeated, as though needing the reassurance.

"Nothing's going to touch us here in Blueberry Springs. I promise."

CATHERINE WAS ON EDGE, and since she knew Zach had noticed, she tried to pass her jumpiness off as simple concern over Xavier. She desperately wanted to believe Zach's words that nothing would touch her here. That she was safe. That what was happening a world away would stay there, far away from her.

Still feeling antsy, she peeked around the edge of the curtain covering the front window. She was getting paranoid, and felt as though she was being watched. Had felt that way for several days. She dropped the curtain and wrapped her arms around herself, shivering as she turned from the window.

She was living a new life, far away from her old one. There was no reason for anyone to come after her even if they found a trail that led them here. She had nothing for them, wasn't to blame, and hoped they knew it.

She needed to act normal or she was going to ruin things between her and Zach.

But her family's associates could easily believe that she'd been an insider, an informant. She'd made her thoughts about their lifestyle clear over the years, and the fact that she'd been brought in only to be released so quickly could be construed as suspicious. What if Jerry had escaped jail because he was motivated by the urge to issue payback? Her cousin had come by his nickname—Bucket—honestly, as everyone who'd crossed him kicked the bucket soon after.

What if... *No. Don't think about Bucket. Don't*

think about Simon. Don't think about what might have happened to have caused his accident or why.

Focus on this life. Today. Xavier. What you have.

And in some ways, she had everything. Xavier was on the mend, thanks to Zach and his willingness to stand out in the late November cold in nothing but boxers and a blanket, her son against his chest as he cared for him like a father.

Catherine felt a warm swelling in her own chest when she thought about Zach and all he was willing to do for her and her son.

This right here was what mattered. This right here was what she needed to focus on, not the ghosts from her past.

*C*atherine still felt as though her past was following her, haunting her, making her a liar. It wasn't a new feeling, but she was tired of it. Tired of believing her cousin Bucket was coming for payback. Tired of watching the shadows. Tired of worrying what others thought.

It was time to hold her head high and own it, quit cowering. She *was* a world away. She'd done a fine job of erasing her steps. All she had to do was continue to avoid the limelight and social media in case Bucket was indeed searching for her, and everything would be fine. She wouldn't have to dart off in the night, making use of her diaper bag's emergency on-the-run items. She wouldn't have to leave Zach in order to protect him from her past.

She was safe here and Xavier was thriving. Plus

she also had a handsome man sleeping on the living room couch, with her son stretched across his chest.

Placing the grocery bags down gently inside the door, she bounded into the living room, then paused, unsure what she should do to the sleeping guys.

"Wake up, sleepyhead," she whispered to Zach. "We have a turkey to cook."

Zach's eyes opened and his lips curved lazily. He went to stretch, but she stopped him, heart racing. "Xavier's on your chest."

"Just seeing how fast your reflexes were." He gave her a cheeky grin and carefully cradled Xavier as he stood, her son's little wet mouth slack against Zach's collarbone. Catherine had to admit she was a tad envious. Being in the shelter of his arms out on the patio last week while settling Xavier's croup had felt good, felt right. She needed to figure out how to get in on more of that.

"It stopped snowing," she said.

"Want to run out and get pie fixings? The car keys are around here somewhere."

"I went out while you were sleeping. I only ran into a few things while figuring out winter driving like you showed me." She began listing incidents, checking them off on her fingers. "There was the car in the parking lot that came around a snowbank too fast, and I didn't have time to brake as I was driving on the wrong side of the road again. I slid down the driveway and took out the garbage cans across the street, but they were plastic so it's okay. And then there was a light post on Main Street. Really, a silly place to have it…"

Zach simply rolled his eyes, knowing she was teasing him. He'd taken her out a few days prior to give her a lesson, and at the time she hadn't known if she was more nervous about being at the wheel of an out-of-control car spinning around on the clear ice of Blueberry Lake, or the fact that Xavier was being watched by the neighbor. She'd never left him alone with anyone other than Zach, and that had occurred only once, this past week. Now twice.

"I've never done Thanksgiving before," she said. "I'm pretty excited."

"It's a lot of cooking and a lot of leftovers."

"Perfect. Less for us to cook later in the week."

"You won't be saying that after four days of turkey this and turkey that."

They set to work in the kitchen, prepping the food while elbow to elbow, laughing and singing to oldies on the radio. It felt warm, homey, and like everything she'd ever wanted.

She'd decided to let go of her past and just relish the fact that everything felt brighter.

"You seem chipper," Zach said a few hours later, as she wiped her brow with an oven mitt. Xavier was still sleeping upstairs. The potatoes were almost ready for mashing, and the apple pie had been squeezed into the oven beside the turkey, which they'd managed to wrangle into a too-small roaster first thing. It was starting to smell delicious, the bird's juices hissing as they hit the sides of the hot pan, making the kitchen area a sensory delight.

"I am chipper." She tapped Zach lightly with the oven mitt. She was pleasantly tired, and had loved every second of cooking with him.

He raised his eyebrows and handed her a glass of nonalcoholic wine, lightly tapping his glass of merlot against it in a silent toast.

"So? What are you thankful for this Thanksgiving?" he asked. He was watching her as they took a sip of their drinks, and seemed to have noticed the shift in her mood and how she'd dropped her paranoia. He seemed relieved, as though her being on edge had put him on edge as well.

"Do people really do that? Make a public gratitude list?" She took a sip of the sweet wine.

"Well, it depends how emotionally needy they are."

Catherine snorted wine out her nose.

"You are so very proper and British, as well as

189

ladylike," Zach said with an amused smile, handing her a cloth to wipe her face.

"This was actually the hardest thing to master in finishing school," she said seriously.

"I'll bet."

She paused, her left arm across her waist as she held her wineglass at chest level with her right. "In an attempt to err on the side of not being emotionally needy, how many things am I safe to list?"

There were so many, how could she choose?

"I was just kidding. Us army guys have trouble with the emotional stuff sometimes. List as much as you'd like."

"Gratitude shouldn't be difficult, Zach."

"True. Just don't make me cry, okay?"

She rolled her eyes, and he reached out and gave her earlobe an affectionate tug, like he was a middle school boy with a crush. She liked it.

"Oh, I will. You'll be crying like a big ol' baby by the time I'm done."

"Maybe I should go first, so you have an example to follow. Try something simple, like how you're grateful for Xavier's returned health."

"Nope. Ladies first. And no suggestions, although that is a good one." She paused, thinking. She had so many things to be hugely grateful for. Soul-baring things. And that's what this exercise could easily become, because she feared that once she started listing all she was thankful for, everything wonderful in her new life would come spilling out, possibly revealing what she'd left behind.

Plus it might end up being like telling a man on the first date that you loved him, wanted to get married and have his babies. Immediately.

"I can go first," Zach said, after she'd paused for a long moment.

"No, I'll go. I was just thinking what's number one on the list."

She stepped closer to him and placed a hand on his waist, an intimate move she'd seen so many couples do without thought. "I am thankful for you."

There. She hadn't kept going. She'd made it simple. Chosen the one thing that all her other gratitudes stemmed from: Zach.

His eyes were warm as he watched her. He said nothing, letting them have this—a moment. A couple's moment.

"I'm thankful you answered my message," she added.

Oh, no. Here she went. He should have said something. She could feel the pressure building inside her to keep sharing, like a train without brakes on a downhill track. To express the avalanche of emotions and gratitude within her.

"I'm thankful that you welcomed me and my son into your wonderful home and beautiful community." Her voice was growing wobbly with emotion, and Zach's hand slipped around her waist, silently supporting her. "I'm so very thankful for you, Zach. Thank you."

She rose on her tiptoes, lightly dusting his lips with hers so she wouldn't say more, then lowered herself, her eyes fluttering open again. He was watching her, his own eyes dark with emotion. He set his wineglass down, then set hers alongside it before sweeping his arms around her, drawing her so close she could scarcely breathe.

It was perfect. Absolutely perfect.

ZACH'S EYELIDS WERE HEAVY, his lips throbbing. He'd never made out with a woman for as long as he had with Catherine, right here in his kitchen. Their lips had explored, their hands weaving warm patterns as they charted the territory of each other's body.

But as they continued to kiss something kept nudging into his mind. Something was screeching, but it wasn't Xavier. It was a horrible sound and he wished it would stop.

He stole another hungry kiss and slid his fingers back into Catherine's thick locks, memorizing the way she felt in his arms.

The world could take a hike. He was kissing his wife.

His. Wife.

"It's the smoke detector," Catherine said, breaking free long enough to utter the words.

They jumped apart, eyes wide.

Smoke. Fire.

"The baby," he said, and Catherine was off at a run to retrieve Xavier before Zach even discovered the source of the smoke.

It was the oven. Smoke was seeping out the edges of the closed door.

"It's okay," he called, the steadiness in his voice surprising him as he dived toward the stove.

How had he not smelled the smoke? How had he not reacted the very second the smoke detector went off? He'd been a mere five feet from the smoke source, seven from the alarm.

Clutching oven mitts, he ignored the shriek of the smoke detectors, which were now drowning out Xavier's freaked-out cries.

Zach felt unsettled and freaked out, too. He was trained for emergencies, and this minor one had his whole nervous system spinning out.

Because, he thought grimly, it had interrupted him while he'd been doing something very, very important. Something he might not get the chance to do again with his wife, who seemed to have finally relaxed after the croup scare.

This Thanksgiving meal had better be the best he'd ever tasted, because he already resented it.

"Open the doors and windows," he called, shoving his hands into the mitts. Then he grabbed the bubbling-over turkey pan, spilling more of the hot juices in the process and sending a new plume of smoke into the room. He was never going to get those alarms silenced again. He set the turkey on the stove and turned on the overhead fan. With the oven so hot he couldn't clean the bottom of the oven, meaning there was no way to stop the smoke. The fats would have to burn off.

While he'd wired all four smoke detectors together so if one went off, they all went off, at least he hadn't set the system up to call the fire department. That's all he'd need—their teasing about his cooking.

His ears were aching from the shrill screeches coming at him from every direction, and he hated to think how it sounded to poor little Xavier.

Through it all, Zach heard the doorbell ring, and he raced to answer it.

Logan came marching in, and Zach tried to fan the room with the open door, hoping that some of the smoke would drift outside.

"You're cooking? It figures." Logan waved at the smoke, then went to open the patio door to create a cross breeze. "At least this time we aren't stuck in a submarine."

"Order me a set of smoke detectors you can turn off," Zach snapped, flapping a tea towel in front of the detector in the kitchen. "And while you're at it, order me a bigger roaster so things don't spill over again next year."

"Did you wire these into your security system?" Logan asked, as a voice clicked on through the system's speaker. "Yup, you did."

"This is Kashmir from your home security network. Is emergency assistance required?"

"No, Zach's just cooking," Logan said with a smirk.

"Is there a fire present?" Kashmir asked. The smoke detectors suddenly went silent and Zach's whole head practically rang in relief.

He caught a glimpse of Catherine standing at the foot of the stairs, Xavier in her arms, his one ear against her chest, her hand pressed to the other one. Her hair was disheveled and her lips plump and swollen from their kisses. Zach's whole world felt as though it shifted, and a flare of heat rose within him as he looked at his wife.

"Is there a fire present?" Kashmir repeated.

Logan, who had noticed the glance they shared,

said, "Looks like these flames are going to be the kind the fire department can't put out."

Zach couldn't agree more.

CATHERINE TRIED to keep her focus on their Thanksgiving dinner guests, as well as on Xavier, who was cooing in the baby swing between her and Zach at the corner of the table. Anything but focus on Zach, because every time she did she felt her cheeks heat, and she'd catch herself touching her lips, curious what it would feel like to kiss him regularly, to allow herself to truly let go and be his wife to the fullest extent.

Ginger was asking her something, and Catherine reached over to give Xavier's windup swing another twist of its dial, to put it back in motion. Something warm and sure was already adjusting the device, and she jerked as a sizzle tingled up her arm at the shared touch. Zach's steady gaze met hers and she tipped her head down, feeling overcome by an inexplicable shyness. She was an adult! She was *married*. It was definitely okay to be attracted to Zach. But it felt like the attraction had just blasted out of left field and taken her down.

"Catherine?" Ginger asked. By the hint of amusement in the woman's tone, Catherine could tell she'd been trying to catch her attention for some time.

"Sorry?"

"Is this your first Thanksgiving?"

"In America?"

"Anywhere."

"Yes. It's very lovely." She winced at her proper tone, the pat, polite British reply. "Other than the whole smoke detector thing," she added, causing her guests, Logan, Ginger, Amy and Moe, to break into laughter.

They'd managed to get the oven to stop smoking, and the meal had turned out well despite the small delay. Xavier, however, was still a bit jumpy thanks to the shrill alarm, even though it had shut off nearly an hour and a half ago. But he was settling, thanks to Zach. Whenever the man held him, said hello on his way by the swing, or tickled his toes, Xavier gave him a toothless grin.

She knew the feeling. It was like there was a force field around Zach that put every sense on high alert when he was near, causing her to hone in on him, become aware of where he was, what he was doing, and whether or not he was looking at her.

Like right now, she knew he was gazing at her because her body was tingling with warmth that was like gooey, freshly made butterscotch.

"How are you finding it, working for the boys?" Ginger asked.

Catherine pulled her head from the clouds, determined to be a better hostess. Her focus so far had most definitely not been on the bounty loading down the table, or their guests.

"It's lovely," she said, and sighed at herself. Another conversation-ending reply. "I'm sorry, I'm not being a very good host. It was a busy day."

Ginger and Logan shared a look and Ginger swallowed a smile. "We'll help clear the table so you and Zach can head to bed early and get your rest."

"Oh, no. You're our guests," Catherine said, standing with her plate. "We insist you relax and allow us to take care of the cleanup." She reached for Ginger's plate, and the woman gave her an odd frown.

Zach reached out and touched her elbow and her breath caught in her throat. "Catherine? We're not done eating."

Ginger laughed as Catherine promptly sat, surprised and embarrassed to see that was true.

"Don't worry," Ginger said. "We can tell you have a lot on your mind. We'll be out of your hair soon."

Catherine was mortified that her crush, or

whatever it was, was not only interfering with everyone's good time, but that it was so obvious.

Ginger leaned closer and said, "You make a great match. *Enjoy* it."

Now she wanted to vanish.

"Tell me about your bridal shop," she said. "I heard Devon's wife makes one-of-a-kind dresses for you?"

Ginger's eyes lit up. "You're in need of a dress for the reception in December?"

"Oh...no. I'm not in need." The reception had been pushed back to December 17, and she still had hopes they could avoid the event altogether.

"You have one already?" The light in Ginger's eyes died and Catherine felt horrible.

"I meant... I don't know that it's...that we're having a reception."

"You have to," Amy insisted from her spot across the table.

"Everything has already been booked," Ginger said, and Amy nodded in agreement.

"Everyone in town is so excited," Amy explained. "December is always cold and dark. We need a reason to party—in a fun way—before we have to spend time with our families for the holidays." She turned to Moe. "Speaking of which, did you find a gift for your dad?"

"Other than paying his mortgage? No."

Amy's shoulders sagged. "He's so impossible to buy for. He needs everything, but makes such a fuss about the cost." She turned back to Catherine. "So? Reception? Yes?" She nodded with a big smile, as if her enthusiasm might cause Catherine to give in.

A reception would be lovely, but so much work in such a short period of time, and it felt...like pretend. Like they were jumping the gun. She knew that didn't make sense, seeing as they were already married, but the party felt like they would be celebrating something the two of them didn't have.

She sneaked a glance at Zach, who was quietly listening, his expression unreadable. To the best of her knowledge their plan still was to find a way to slip out of the commitment.

Catherine had opened her mouth to argue the value of holding a reception when Ginger said quickly, cutting her off, "Are you big into the holidays? I love Christmas and try to go all out, especially now that I know Annabelle loves the holiday, too."

"Where is she tonight?" Amy asked.

"She has a boyfriend," Ginger sang.

"Somehow —" Logan gave Ginger a pointed look "—she convinced me it was okay for her to forgo dinner with us and spend it with her boyfriend's family."

"So? What are your plans?" Ginger asked, waving off Logan. "This is Xavier's first Christmas. Are you going to do it up big?"

Memories of Catherine's own Christmases came to mind. The new bicycle—which she later discovered had been stolen from a girl in her grade who lived one block over. The holiday trips where her father took them to exotic locales, and upon arrival back at the British border she'd be questioned heavily about what all her father had done while away, where he'd gone, who he'd seen, where they'd stayed and what all was in the suitcase upturned on the counter in front of them. The month of December was always filled with big, loud celebrations where her father pulled out his accordion and played for their guests, the house filling with music and the sound of singing. But as the night wore on, as her father and his associates drank too much, brawls would inevitably break out, destroying the feelings of warmth and joy that had been building all night. Since Catherine had left home, Christmas had been a quiet nonevent, one where she hoped her favorite takeout place would remain open for the holiday.

"I like a quiet Christmas," she said. Compared to the fuss she'd grown up with, she definitely preferred something peaceful and low-key.

"I do, too," Zach stated, and Catherine almost

wished he'd said the opposite. "It's all I've ever known."

"Big ones are just more stress, more stuff, more expectation, more fights and more disappointment," Catherine said, a bit too forcefully. She inhaled and tried for a smile, putting her focus on Xavier in hopes that the sudden welling up in her eyes would go unnoticed. She'd always envied families who seemed to have these wonderful cozy Christmases filled with love and joy. Despite the unorthodox relationship she had with Zach, she hoped to be able to build traditions for Xavier that he looked forward to, cherished times where he felt part of something special.

"So we keep it low-key," Zach said.

"Low-key," she confirmed.

She dared cut a glance toward Zach and voice what she believed he was thinking. "You want a big one."

"Nah."

"You do."

"I want low-key." He paused for a split second. "What *is* low-key?"

"Presents within your price range."

"Smart."

"One or two outings over the holidays."

"You don't want to wear yourself out," he agreed, nodding thoughtfully.

"You bake a few cookies for yourself and the neighbors. Little treats that are special and fun to make."

"I like cookies."

"Just clean that oven before you start," Logan interrupted with a laugh.

"Not too many parties, or presents. And you don't give gifts to every person you know," Catherine continued, not deterred from the vision filling her imagination.

"No need to go overboard and be a show-off."

The month of December for her father had always meant a lot of envelopes, some thicker than others, as he made the rounds, glad-handing his associates, doling out bonuses to his most loyal lackeys. He came home with enough of those filled envelopes for himself, bribes and payments for granting his protection to businesses around the neighborhood, that he could have bought her the stolen bike, plus a few more for luck. Pushing aside her bitterness, Catherine focused on her Christmas Day dream for her and Xavier. It was simple, but exactly what she felt the holiday should be.

"Christmas morning is when the kids wake you up, thrilled that Santa has arrived. You're in your housecoat, sipping a cup of coffee, as you watch them open their stockings. Then have a delicious British breakfast of bangers and mash sometime before or after they open the gifts." She could feel it. The sense of calm contentment. "On Christmas morning you have all the time in the world to cozy up on the couch with the person you love, while your children unwrap their presents, their eyes lit up with joy. There's nothing you have to do that day. Just sit and enjoy your family in the peace and calm of the season, mindful of what you have in your life. There are always so many blessings to count."

"I like it," Zach said softly. "Let's do that. It can become our tradition." He leaned close, giving her a soft kiss on the lips.

ZACH LEANED back in his chair, satisfied and happy. The meal had been amazing, even though the pie's crust had tasted a bit like smoked turkey, thanks to the grease and smoke that had enveloped it while it had been baking alongside the meat. He looked around the table at his friends, his wife and Xavier. The full stomach, good meal, laughter and fun-loving company all felt right.

This was real life. This was living.

And he liked it.

He was also pretty tickled with how Catherine kept sneaking shy glances his way, her cheeks pinking. If he didn't know any better he would say his wife had a crush on him.

That idea made him smile.

And that sweet kiss after she'd shared a perfect Christmas dream with him... Life couldn't be much better. Especially since her dream had included snuggling on the couch with the person she loved—could that one day be him?—and watching her kids open gifts. Yes, plural. As in more than one child. Somewhere along the line she planned on adding to her family, and he hoped he was the one who fathered them.

Logan lifted one eyebrow slightly, obviously catching the fact that Zach was pretty much sliding down that slippery slope, straight into love. Zach smiled and shrugged, knowing it would be okay. Catherine wasn't going anywhere and neither was he. A few days ago she'd been edgy and antsy, but had since let it go, settling in and allowing herself to become even closer to him. Patience was all he'd needed. Just patience. And he felt now that nothing could come between them, get in the way, or cause this fairy tale to not become a reality.

In his contentment, he found himself saying, despite knowing Catherine was still trying to get out of it, "We should have that reception."

The idea truly had merit.

"Why not?" he asked, when she gave him a dark look for switching sides.

Ginger and Amy didn't dare speak, but their eyes glimmered hopefully as they watched Catherine contemplate Zach.

"It's a ridiculous expense," she said quietly. "And it's not fair for Mary Alice and Liz to pay for it even if they've pushed it on us."

"You could hold it at the pub," Amy said. "Free venue."

Moe shot her a quick look to which she mouthed, *"What?"*

"Aren't the ladies taking care of things though?" Zach asked.

"There's still time to tweak it so you can be certain the event remains low-key." Amy gave a smile that could have belonged on a sly fox. "Why not a wine and cheese on a weekday night? That way it won't get out of hand."

"They hired Lily to make sandwiches," Ginger said. "And trying to convince Mary Alice and Liz to change their plans...good luck with that."

"Great. So we're doing finger sandwiches, wine and cheese in the pub," Amy replied.

"If you say so," Ginger said out the side of her mouth.

"Trust me. I know what to say to Richard to ensure he's got the community center *accidentally* double-booked."

"There's no way he'll mess with Mary Alice and her plans."

"He will for Nicola. He owes her one for a booking mishap during one of her Valentine's events."

Ginger shrugged. "Worth trying."

Zach tipped his head, watching Catherine. He could see she was a little bit tempted, by the way she was chewing on her bottom lip.

"I know our marriage isn't a traditional one," he said carefully, aware that what he was about to say could blow up in his face. "But why not celebrate it anyway? We've decided we can handle being around each other. Maybe we could get a little photo to put on the mantel to show Xavier he's part of a family."

Zach focused on refilling his guests' wineglasses, knowing it wasn't fair to play the family-for-her-son card. Maybe it was the wine, maybe it was her kisses that he couldn't seem to stop thinking about, maybe it was his full stomach, the warm house and sense of contentment. But the fact was he finally felt as though he was part of something—real life—and he wanted to celebrate it. He wanted to stand on the steps in front of the church and yell out to the town how wonderful Catherine was. Just like he'd heard Oz Reiter had years ago, when he'd been struggling with sobriety and had lost the love of his life.

Although maybe wanting to stand on the steps and potentially humiliate himself said more about the amount of wine he'd been drinking and less about how full of life he felt.

He shook off the thought that he might be jumping into things.

"Would the ladies organizing be satisfied with something like that?" Catherine asked. "I wouldn't want to step on their toes or upset them." She was keeping her attention directed toward Xavier, lightly toying with his toes.

"Some will grumble that it isn't a full feast." Ginger laughed. "But it's for you. You should have a say."

"I think it'll be fine," Amy said, reassuring Catherine.

"Excellent," Zach said. "Consider it decided. When should we do this? Same date as the ladies had booked?"

Catherine shot him a panicked look, and he said smoothly, "It's all good. I'll talk to them."

"Is a weekend okay or does it need to be a weeknight?" he asked Amy.

"No problem. I've got it handled," she replied. "Will you two sing?" She turned to Ginger. "These two can sing a duet like you would not *believe*. They could win a reality show, hands down."

Ginger narrowed her eyes at Zach. "You are *so* full of secrets."

"Secret talents, you mean?"

"Catherine suggested we seed our next karaoke night with professionals," Amy said.

"Not professionals," Catherine pointed out, "just people who make patrons feel inspired to get up there and belt it out."

"You know a lot about pub events," Moe said. "With the baby coming in the next few months, we could use some help organizing things. Nicola Samuels-Haber from the town office used to run a few events using the pub as a venue. Since having the twins and shifting to part-time, she hasn't been as involved and we're noticing the difference. I know you're not interested in helping with the accounting, but maybe you could come in for a few hours each month to help organize some fun?"

"Oh, I don't know," Catherine said.

"We could really use help brainstorming, if nothing else," Amy said, rubbing circles over her stretched stomach.

"I can guarantee there's nothing illegal happening under the table at Brew Babies," Zach said quietly, figuring that could be part of why she was feeling gun-shy.

"Well, there might be kissing, but that's entirely legal," Logan said with a laugh. "What if you had a local talent night? You could charge admission."

"Who would pay admission to hear their neighbors sing?" Zach asked.

"Just trying to come up with ideas," Logan grumbled, leaning back. His phone buzzed and he pulled it out to read a message.

"I'd pay to hear these two," Amy said, pointing to Zach and Catherine.

"Maybe a jug and jam?" Catherine suggested. She described the event where local musicians came in to play and people joined in or bought them jugs of beer as a thanks for the entertainment.

Before long Amy, Moe and Catherine were deep into new ideas on how they could bring in more patrons with little effort and little overhead.

Logan tipped closer to Zach, saying under his breath, so Catherine wouldn't hear, "Scott's hoping we can look over some evidence from one of the recent break-ins."

"There've been more?"

Logan nodded.

"Yeah, let's end that spree."

Logan texted the officer back. It wasn't uncommon for Scott to reach out to them as contractors to provide an extra set of eyes on tougher cases. While Scott had finally received a backup officer in town after arresting Spencer Phipps for messing with things over at Brew Babies, thanks to help from Zach and Logan last summer, the new recruit was fresh out of the academy and didn't have the experience the two of them had. He'd get there, but it would take time.

Catherine was laughing, and Amy, her eyes lit up, was saying, "You don't think a town like Blueberry Springs could handle some male strippers?"

"No way," Moe said, arms crossed, jaw set. "Not in my pub."

"Just one night," Catherine said, shooting Amy a look that sent the pregnant woman into giggles. It seemed as if Catherine had not only found herself another part-time job, but a new friend, too.

"The pub is only *half* yours," Amy told her husband as she placed a hand on her belly. "Oh! The baby just kicked. I think that's a vote for the strippers."

"I think it's kicking the idea to the curb," Moe said, leaning forward to kiss his wife.

Zach glanced at Catherine, who was watching them with a wistful expression. Despite what she might sometimes say, he knew that she was looking for the kind of thing Amy and Moe had. And so was he.

11

As Catherine wrapped a cheery red-and-white woolly scarf knitted by Gran around her neck, she mulled over how she felt like she was already a part of the town despite having been in Blueberry Springs for slightly less than a month. Everyone—including the rampant gossips—had been kind and generous, and nobody seemed to have expectations that she repay them. Of course, Catherine had tried to express her gratitude by being helpful and generous, as well, but most of her offers had been gently rebuffed.

However, last night at their Thanksgiving dinner, she hadn't meant to offer her help to Amy and Moe. But she'd found herself getting swept up in the thrill of new publicity ideas, and before long their genuine love of her customer-centric approach had led to a second part-time job.

She'd been both tired and wired last night, wound tight over Zach and his kisses, and unsure what the night would bring. But right after supper, Zach had gone out with Logan to take care of some work, coming home hours after she'd expected him to. She knew he could take care of himself, but there had been a series of break-ins lately and it worried her that he was out on a job. And not just for his sake, but hers, too, in case his home was targeted by the thieves despite the state-of-the-art security system.

But today was time for fun, not worries. Zach, who said he needed to be out of the house so he wasn't tempted to spend his way into the red with today's Black Friday online shopping deals, had persuaded her to join him and some friends in heading up into the mountains to select a real tree to bring home and decorate for Christmas. Even though it was only the end of November, the whole town seemed to be in full preparation mode already, stringing up decorations and preparing for the holidays. Catherine had said yes to the tree idea, excited to start new traditions with both Xavier and Zach.

She had just finished zipping Xavier into his snowsuit when Zach came in the front door, where he'd been out shoveling yet more snow. "I have a sled with a little seat for Xavier and a flat one for the tree."

He came near, watching her to make sure it was okay before placing a soft kiss on her forehead. She appreciated that he was careful, but even more, she liked that he kissed her.

And she'd like it even more if he kissed her a little longer and on the lips.

She grabbed the front of Zach's coat before he could step away, pulling him in for a kiss.

She released him with a happy sound and he smiled, dropping another kiss on her lips. If she wasn't careful they'd never get out of the house. Since cooking the turkey—which had indeed supplied them with ample leftovers—they'd been acting a little more like a real married couple than simple flatmates. Kisses here and there, a little hand holding while watching the morning news. It was nice. Really nice. And she appreciated that Zach was taking it slow, letting their feelings catch up with their desire before pressing forward. Even though she wanted to go faster.

"How far will we be hiking?" she asked, following him into the garage with Xavier.

"Depends how far we have to go to find the prefect tree."

Catherine thought about the large mountains

that surrounded the town, so tall and imposing. But more than that, she'd mistakenly stepped off the packed, snowy path while taking a shortcut along the river the day before yesterday and had landed in thigh-deep snow, causing her to panic. She couldn't imagine there would be a wide and well-packed trail leading to their "perfect" tree, which meant she'd be struggling through deep snow today and trying not to imagine being buried alive in the fluffy stuff.

"Not too far, I hope," she said, as she set the house's alarm before closing the door to the garage. "Maybe we can find something near the road?"

Zach amused her with a "maybe." Once they were in the SUV, he said, "Jill Armstrong's bringing a small breakfast picnic for everyone, so we probably won't starve. She works for Emma's cosmetic company in that new log building out past the downtown. I don't think you've met her."

"Is anyone bringing a rescue dog?"

"Jill will probably bring Taylor, who's a Great Pyrenees, but I wouldn't count on that dog rescuing you. Taylor's pretty chill."

A few minutes later they were in the meadow parking lot just across the river, where a few people were milling about in the sunshine as though the cold didn't bother them. Which possibly it didn't.

"Hey, you guys!" Amy called, waving them over, her large coat barely closing over her stomach. "What kind of tracks are these?" She pointed to the snow.

Catherine came a bit closer, tugging the sled with the little baby seat, which had Xavier propped up in it.

Zach apparently needed just a glance before declaring it a wolf track.

"Are you certain it's not just a dog?" Catherine asked, gesturing toward a massive white dog off-leash and romping across the meadow.

"I'm always sure," he replied.

"Men. So overconfident," Amy said. She rolled her eyes and carefully made her way across the parking lot to talk to Logan and Ginger about which trail to take up the mountainside. It turned out a lot of people snowshoed and hiked the nearby trails, giving them a choice of mostly firm paths to stay on until they found their tree. Catherine hoped it would be safe enough for the mom-to-be.

"We're not overconfident," Zach said. "We're just awesome. Why can't women see that?"

Catherine gave him a playful shove, laughing as he pretended she'd pushed him harder than she had, and tumbled into the drift at the edge of the parking lot, just about disappearing into the fluffy snow.

"You sink like a rock," she said, offering him a hand.

"It's all this muscle." He gave a swift yank, tugging her on top of him. As she fell, she dropped the sled's rope so as not to pull Xavier along with her. She landed on Zach, squealing as flakes of snow puffed up, dusting her face and feeling similar to a cold London drizzle as they melted against her skin.

"You sink like a rock, too, Mrs. Forrester," Zach murmured, his warm lips welcome against her cheek as he blazed a hot trail across it. Her entire being warmed at being called that, for being someone who belonged with this wonderful, kind and funny man.

"Careful there, buster," she said, trying not to show just how much she loved being "Mrs. Forrester."

"Or what?" His arms tightened around her waist. "You don't like being called Mrs.?"

"I do like it." She risked meeting his gaze, and when she did it was as though every wall she'd ever had came tumbling down. In that moment it was just her and him, nothing hidden.

She pushed herself off him, frightened by how it felt to be unprotected, scared that it might be okay to be so vulnerable and exposed with someone.

Could she really be his? Truly his?

"Are you planning to keep me here until I freeze to death?" she asked, as she struggled to get out of the drift and failed.

"I can think of a few ways to keep us both warm."

She laughed and allowed herself to tumble back against him.

"Newlyweds," Logan muttered to Ginger as they passed by.

"Hand up?" Zach asked, reaching past Catherine.

"I think we should leave *you* here in the snow," Catherine said, reaching for Logan in turn.

Instead of taking her offered hand, he clutched Zach's. "Hold on, mate. You, too, my little sheila."

With a sharp pull, he lifted Zach out of the drift, Catherine clinging to him and coming along for the ride.

"My word," she said to Logan once she was on her feet. "You must be able to bench-press a train."

Ginger snuggled against her husband, looking up with a smile. Zach rolled his eyes as the two of them kissed, and Catherine giggled, knowing that at the moment they weren't much better than the happy couple.

And she wouldn't change it for the world.

ZACH LOVED that Catherine was enjoying the hike. She seemed to savor all the same things he did, from the fresh air to any excuse to hold her in his arms. His favorite was to stand behind her, one arm around her waist as he leaned in close, so he could line up his other arm like a sight for her eyes to track toward a potential tree higher up the mountain. He was pretty sure Catherine was onto him, since every tree he'd chosen had been awful, but she didn't seem to mind the game.

Up here he felt as though he could focus on real life rather than the puzzle that had defeated Logan, Scott and himself last night. They'd been sitting in the large log structure that served as the town's police station, quietly sorting through Scott's meager evidence from last week's break-ins, when a call had come in for another forced entry. They'd gone out as soon as Scott was off the phone, trying to catch up with the thieves as they hit three places in a row.

The three of them had spread out, confident they'd meet with success in this small town they knew so well. At one point Zach had thought he saw seen someone on foot, but by the time he reached the end of the street in his Land Rover, the shadows were empty.

He'd gone home hours later, defeated, his mind buzzing with details that wouldn't triangulate into anything solid enough to offer Scott as a possible lead. Catherine had been up feeding Xavier and had wanted to chat, but Zach, feeling bad, had slipped away at the first opportunity so he could sit down in his office and think.

But today was about him and Catherine, as well as himself, Catherine and Xavier as a family. Zach's heart expanded in his chest, a bubble of happiness ballooning inside him. There was something about Catherine that allowed them to connect. With her it felt as though he had enough to give, and that what he did give she cherished and appreciated. Flaws and all.

Catching up with her and Xavier again, he dropped the cable for his own sled and picked her up, swinging her in a circle, even though it meant the two of them would get wrapped in the cord of Xavier's sled. He buried his face in her scarf, burrowing to the flesh of her neck so he could kiss her, inhale her. He held her close and her body softened into his.

"How did I ever find you?" she asked, when he put her down again.

"Best online shopping day of my life."

She laughed and playfully patted his chest with her mitten.

He glanced to the side to snag a visual of Xavier, who was still right side up in his little sled despite the way Zach had just spun his mother around. Then his attention was right back on Catherine and those gorgeous blue eyes that were filled with so much wonder, peace, and happiness. He had put that there. He had made her smile, relax. She had let him in.

"Let this new custom of ours mark the beginning of what will surely be a long and wonderful marriage," he said, brushing a wisp of hair off her cheek.

Together, they had everything they needed, that special thing nobody else had been able to offer.

In fact, he thought, as he tipped his head down for a sweet kiss, it just might be perfect.

———

CATHERINE FELT as if she flapped her arms she could lift off and fly above the alpine meadows. In one month her life had gone from a nightmare to a fantasy. Zach was wonderful—with her, with Xavier. She felt safe and relaxed, certain in the knowledge that he wouldn't judge her, as she had been in the past.

And yet she felt there was no point in telling him every little thing about her childhood. They understood each other as they were in this moment, and that was enough for right now. She was being the woman she had always wanted to be. One she never thought she'd get the chance to be. Happy and safe, living the good life with a precious, beautiful and healthy baby boy. And right now that meant enjoying a picnic with new friends, all satisfied with their Christmas tree choices.

Catherine hooked her arm through Zach's, surprising him as she clinked her metal cup of hot chocolate against his before raising it to her lips. There were six of them, herself and Zach, Ginger and Logan, and Jill and Burke, gathered in a circle on the mountain, Amy and Moe having already headed back to the car after selecting their tree.

"You forgot to make a toast," Zach said quietly.

She paused before her sip. "To new beginnings."

"To new beginnings and new marriages," he replied, taking a sip of his own hot chocolate.

They kissed, warm, sweet and chocolaty.

"How did I get so lucky?" she murmured.

"How did *I*?" he replied.

"Come on, you guys," Jill said. "You're going to make everyone barf their picnic breakfast all over this pristine snow."

Her husband coughed, spraying out his mouthful of cocoa.

Catherine laughed. Jill, with her strong build, came off as a tough woman, but had a gentle soul and a sense of humor that had tickled Catherine as they'd watched and joked as the men struggled through the waist-deep snow to cut the chosen trees.

"Do you have a cast-iron skillet in need of seasoning?" Jill asked. "Ginger and I are getting ours done." Ginger nodded in agreement.

Catherine gave them a puzzled look, wondering why they wouldn't just do it themselves.

Jill and Ginger simultaneously began fanning their faces. Okay, so the pan seasoner was dreamy. *Got it.*

She laughed as Logan said, "This is our cue, boys."

Burke and Zach stood, heading farther up the path to secure the last tree on a sled. As Zach passed Catherine and Xavier, who was sitting in his own sled, he unstrapped the baby boy and picked him up, carrying him on his hip.

A family.

That's what she now had.

"So?" Jill prodded. "Do you need yours done? If we can collect over ten orders we get a 20 percent discount. He comes to town once a year and seasons cast-iron pans and sharpens knives. Burke was ready to toss out his knife set and this guy brought it back to life for only a couple bucks. He does it that day in his truck."

"I'll ask Zach," Catherine said.

"Let either of us know if you're in," Ginger said.

"Okay."

"Did you hear about that break-in near you?" Jill asked Catherine, who shook her head. "It was just a few streets over from your place."

"Don't freak her out," Ginger scolded.

"I'm not." Jill laughed. "Everything's a few streets over in Blueberry Springs. And you're the one who should be freaked out because you live even closer. And anyway, Catherine has a security system—"

"So do I," Ginger said.

"—as well as a big burly man keeping her warm at night."

Catherine ignored the comment, hoping she wasn't blushing. She and Zach weren't quite at the keeping-each-other-warm-at-night stage.

"Again, so do I," Ginger said with a dry tone.

"We don't need details about you ladies and your James Bonds," Jill retorted.

"Wasn't going to give them." Ginger's expression became somber and she looked up the hill toward the men.

"James Bonds?" Catherine laughed.

"Because they're in security," Ginger said quickly, cutting off Jill, who gave her a funny look.

"They hit three places in one night," Jill said soberly. "I've been sleeping with my gun under my pillow."

"Your gun?" Catherine asked in surprise. Sure, her father had slept that way, but the general British population did not. Over here, she realized, things were different, but she hadn't expected Jill to be the gun-sporting type.

"My dad owns the gun range in town."

"She's a sharpshooter," Ginger explained. "Used to win competitions and stuff."

"Really?" Catherine reassessed the woman

"Totally into being a female Rambo," Ginger said.

Jill rolled her eyes. "If you want to learn how to shoot a gun, come to me. I'll teach you."

"I don't think…" Catherine, who'd grown up around guns and never been comfortable with them, much to her father's confusion, couldn't imagine keeping herself armed. Not even when she'd been on the run had she carried anything other than mace. But maybe she should. The culture around weapons was different here than it was in England and she might be smart to consider it. "I'll think about it."

Jill smiled.

"When did they break in?" Catherine asked, wondering if it was while she'd been home alone with Xavier.

"Between ten and two last night," Ginger said.

Catherine struggled to turn her mind away from the avenue it wanted to go down. Zach had indeed been out during those hours, and he'd been oddly silent when he'd come home, preferring to lock himself in his office instead of talking.

"Was Logan out last night?" she asked.

"He was with Zach," Ginger said slowly. "When did he come home?"

"Around two."

"That's when Logan came home." Ginger wasn't watching her, but concentrating on packing away the remains of their picnic. Catherine got a strange feeling that she was hiding something.

Jill popped to her feet and went to collect her off-leash dog, who was greeting hikers coming up the path.

"He's a good man," Ginger said, raising her eyes to meet Catherine's. "You can trust him."

"Zach? Or Logan?"

"Both," she said firmly.

"How can I be sure?"

"Because you can trust *me*. And I know them both."

Catherine only wished it was that easy. Because there was one thing that never came easily for her, and that was trust.

———

ZACH HAD to admit he was pretty proud of their Christmas tree. Not only would it add an incredible smell to their home, adding spice to the holiday season, but it also marked the beginning of a new life.

Dragging the tree on the sled, Zach came up beside Catherine as they approached the parking lot and the path widened out. She'd gone quietly contemplative on the walk down the mountain, and he couldn't help but notice the questions in her eyes whenever they met his.

He considered placing a kiss on her cheek, but there was barely an inch skin exposed, given the dropping temperature, and burrowing into her scarf to kiss her neck like he had earlier didn't feel right somehow.

"What did you think of selecting our own tree?" He glanced back, making sure his oversized load wasn't bumping into Catherine's sled, which held Xavier. Overhead, an eagle was circling, dipping and weaving as it rode the air currents.

"It was wonderful." She stopped walking, then

reached over and placed a mittened hand against his cheek, watching him for a long moment. He felt as though she was reassessing him somehow. "I hope this is the beginning of many new traditions for our family."

Our family.

His worries about the way she'd gone quiet on the walk flew from his mind and his heart soared like the eagle circling above.

"Me, too," he replied huskily, relieved by her words. He needed to remember that sometimes people got freaked out when their baby got sick, or that sometimes they simply needed some space to be alone with their thoughts.

She dropped her hand and turned away, her thoughtful expression returning as they headed to the SUV.

Zach unlocked the vehicle for Catherine and began untying the tree from the sled so he could put it on the roof of his Land Rover.

"Hey, Logan?" Zach squatted in the snow, working on the knots.

Logan, a few cars down, turned.

"Think I could just tie this whole thing to the bumper and drag it back to town?" His fingers were already seizing up from being exposed to the cold and wind as he worked to loosen the ropes.

"Only if Scott isn't looking," Logan replied. "I don't think that's a legal trailer."

Zach let out an amused grunt and continued working on freeing the tree.

"Did you want your knives sharpened and cast-iron pan seasoned?" Catherine asked, bringing him Xavier's empty sled, having put him in the Land Rover. "Jill was asking."

Zach shrugged. What did he know about that stuff? He'd been in charge of grills and pots of boiling water for the first year or two in the army, not anything technical. But if it made his wife happy, it made him happy. And he was all about happy. "Sure."

"I'll let her know." Catherine headed over to where Ginger and Jill were chatting. "Can you keep an ear out for Xavier?" She gestured to the vehicle.

"Sure." Zach watched her go, glad that she didn't seem to be rebuilding her walls. She was nearly back to what he considered her regular self again.

Patience, he reminded himself. That was all she and their relationship needed.

She'd been through a lot in the past year with the stalker, losing her baby's father, as well as being rounded up as a suspect at the nightclub. Not to mention motherhood, a new husband and moving to a foreign country. That was enough to send anyone into moments of mental retreat even with someone they trusted.

Shortly after, Catherine rejoined him, asking, "Do you have your cell phone?"

The wind had picked up, throwing snow at them.

"Yeah. You need it?" He really needed to get her set up with one, but she kept insisting she was fine without one. He had a feeling she'd continue to say no until she could afford to buy one with her own money. Which meant he needed to surprise her with one. Maybe he could claim it was an employee perk, and that Logan had insisted she be connected at all times in case they needed her. She wouldn't accept that as a valid excuse from him, but maybe if Logan delivered it she'd be too polite to refuse.

"There's a man who's locked himself out of his car, and his phone is inside. Can you call a tow truck?"

"Maybe you can help," Logan said, coming over. "Used to be pretty good at that."

Zach shot his friend a dark look. "Just give the guy your phone."

"It died. Too cold on the mountain." He gave Zach a grin and he wasn't sure whether to believe the man or not. Either way, being able to break into vehicles and buildings, as well as sneak around firewalls and various security systems, was not a skill Zach liked to advertise in public. Or to his wife. Especially with the way her shoulders had stiffened beneath her bulky parka at Logan's comment.

Sure, someone was bound to let it slip soon enough that part of his military career had actually evolved into elite intelligence work, which might help explain his skill set in a legal context. But he had a very strong feeling that his past would make Catherine uncomfortable. The silent questions of what all he had done during that career. Who he'd hurt. Who he'd pretended to be. She wouldn't like it.

He just wanted time. Time for her to get to know him better—the true heart of him. Not the labels that could be so easily applied.

"Zach's had a lot of careers," Logan explained to Catherine.

"He makes me sound criminal," Zach told her. "I can give it a shot, but you should probably call Gus."

"Frankie's in the city today," Logan said, referring to the local auto body fanatic who helped the tow truck driver, Gus, from time to time. "Mandy wanted to hit some big designer sale."

"How do you know these things?" Ginger asked,

coming over to join them. "You're worse than the gossips."

"That's why I suggested we call Gus," Zach said slowly and deliberately, as though Logan was having cognitive issues. "Get him to bring his truck and locksmith skills out here."

"Gus fell off his diet wagon last night at his sister's. His gout is something awful today," Logan said, mimicking Zach's tone.

Great. Gus was going to be no use to them.

"Again, you're worse than the gossips," Ginger said. She put an arm out to steer Catherine toward the Land Rover. "Let's wait out of the wind while these two go and save the day."

Looked like they were doing this.

"Don't make it look too easy," Logan muttered under his breath as they walked toward Logan's car.

"Do you think I was born yesterday?"

Logan pulled a small black bag from his trunk. "What's got Catherine so reflective today?"

Zach sighed. "I don't know. I'm trying to be patient, but sometimes it's hard. I have to remind myself she's had a big year."

Logan gave him a grim look. "You might need to come clean about your past life."

"She won't like it."

He closed the trunk, facing Zach. "It's just a matter of time until she finds out."

"I know." And then what? She might believe it was a big oversight of his to not divulge the fact that his military career had involved espionage.

As they walked toward the locked-out hiker, Logan handed Zach the bag of tools he'd need. Old habits died hard. Logan shouldn't need these things in their current career, but Zach understood how hard it was to resist adding all the old tools of the trade into one's personal kit. And if he started riding Logan for his stash, he might have to admit that he had himself similarly equipped.

"My hands are freezing from dealing with those ropes," Zach said. "Distract him so I can pop it fast."

While Logan chatted with the stranded guy, Zach pretended to struggle even after he heard the lock pop a split second after he set to work. The man couldn't see him from where he stood and Zach slipped his mitts back on, warming his fingers. He waited another minute or two, glad the guy couldn't tell he wasn't doing anything.

"You're in," Zach finally announced, his skills making him feel criminal instead of a hero.

"That was fast." The man shook his hand, then Logan's, and thanked them both before diving into the car, finding his keys and starting the engine so he could warm up.

When Zach returned to his Land Rover Catherine was watching him through the passenger side window with an expression he wasn't sure he wanted to read.

Yeah. He was fast. One of the fastest back in training, and one of the fastest out in the field. A tricky door? Give it to Zach. He sent Logan a look as if to say "Thanks a lot, pal."

Logan gave him two thumbs-up with a grin, ignoring Zach's dark look as he opened the door for his wife to climb out of the backseat, where she'd been keeping warm while chatting with Catherine and Xavier. Hand in hand, Logan and Ginger headed to their own car for the ride back to town.

Zach took the driver's seat, waiting for Catherine to say what was surely on her mind.

"You can break into vehicles?" she said, her voice flat, the question a statement.

"It's my job."

"What exactly *is* your job?" She'd turned in her seat to face him, her spine twisted.

"Security." He glanced at her, hoping to convey that he was someone she didn't need to fear or doubt. "I keep people safe. I have to know my way around locks and security systems."

"But how do you know?" Catherine insisted. "Where did you learn?"

"I used to install vehicle security alarms."

Mostly true, although he'd mostly just dismantled them. But he'd once been trained to install them, as his instructor had explained, "If you know how to make them work, you'll know how to make them not work."

They drove in silence for a few minutes and he made a wish that the doubt in her voice would somehow become as easy to disarm as it seemed to have been to install.

"I heard there was another break-in last night," she finally said, as they drove over the bridge into town.

"Three."

"I wish you'd been home."

Zach weighed whether she was worried about being alone during an attempted break-in or whether it was more doubt seeping in. He could practically hear her unasked questions. *Where were you during the robberies last night? Why did you really learn to break into cars? Can you break into homes, too?*

"We have a good security system," he said. "You're safe even when I'm not home."

"What if someone knew their way around the security system or broke in anyway?"

"Scott's working on catching whoever it is." Zach focused on the snowy streets more than he needed to, trying to prevent giving himself away or confessing to his full range of skills. He was used to keeping them secret, and simply turning and telling her everything felt like a breach. He was going to have to figure out how to explain.

"You've known him a long time?"

"I've known Officer Malone as long as I've lived here."

"I heard he's understaffed."

"He is."

"So what do I do if someone tries to force their way in and you're not home?"

Relief allowed Zach's shoulders to relax. She was merely concerned about safety. That was what all this was about.

"I live there," he said with a laugh. "No thief would dare come and mess with *my* home."

When it came to targeting houses, his would be one of the last ones on the list. He was doing everything right, from a highly visible front door to a high-tech security system. His home was not an easy mark. Sure, someone could try and break into it. But a thief worth his salt wouldn't choose his as one to start with.

"Back home, we used to leave our house unlocked."

He felt like she was offering something. A story. A snippet from her past. Something he was supposed to bite on.

"Safe town?"

"The break-ins have been good for your business," she said, changing the subject. It was true. There had been an uptick in security system installations.

But the way she was winding herself tight, that stress from weeks ago cranking up within her, told him her home's unlocked doors weren't because of the town's safety. It was due to something else. And from experience, he figured the safest house in a crime-ridden neighborhood was the crime boss's house.

So was she from a crime family?

Did that explain her preference for morality? His instinct to not reveal his former intelligence training for fear of her pulling away?

Or was he grasping at straws so he wouldn't have to consider that maybe she was retreating because she didn't actually feel they were as good of a fit as he believed?

12

Zach studied the tree, his arms wrapped around the thick branches as Catherine tightened the stand's screws into its trunk. His ability to swiftly enter a locked car had altered the way she viewed him, right before his eyes. Which he understood. How many people knew how to bust into a car, for righteous reasons? She had been burned back at the nightclub, and it made sense that she might be suspicious about things that didn't add up.

He should have called Gus to come out in the cold to deal with the car, despite his gout. But Zach was in it now, and she needed for him to let her in on some truths.

Summoning his courage, he said, "Catherine?"

"Hmm?" She was still under the tree, adjusting the screws.

"Sometimes missions called for me to enter locked vehicles."

She was quiet.

"I'm not used to talking about it," he said awkwardly.

"Okay," she said simply, seeming to accept his answer.

"Okay?"

Catherine crawled out from under the tree and knelt with her hands on her knees. She met his eye and he tentatively released his grip on the tree.

"Yeah. I guess I wasn't expecting you to be able to pop a lock that fast." She looked down at her hands and picked at a fingernail. "I got caught up in my thoughts."

"It's not a common skill," he said supportively. "At least among those who aren't criminals."

She rewarded him with a wan smile and he felt his shoulders relax.

"We're good?" he asked, offering her a hand up.

"Of course we are, Zach."

This whole letting-people-in thing might be all right, after all.

She took a look at the tree. "I think that should do it. The screws were supereasy to turn, though. Think it'll hold?"

Xavier was safely out of the way, sitting in his swing and idly sucking on his fist. Zach stepped back to stand beside him, just as Catherine did, too, and the tree pitched toward the plate glass window behind it. Catherine let out a little squeak as they both lurched to catch the evergreen, getting their palms stabbed with needles.

"Ouch!" Catherine said.

"You all right?"

"We should have bought a fake tree."

He grinned. "Where's the fun in that?" He bent down to retighten the screws, careful not to spill the water in the bottom of the stand.

"It smells good in here, though," Catherine said, as Zach stood up. He agreed. There was nothing like a real tree when it came to infusing the feeling of Christmas into a home—and that's what it was with Catherine and Xavier in it.

She started giggling.

The tree was crooked. And there was a bare spot where a branch was missing.

"I'll turn it around." Zach carefully adjusted the tree so it was more upright and the empty space was facing the wall.

He stood back, arms crossed, as he admired his work.

"Where are your decorations?" Catherine asked.

Zach's arms dropped to his sides. He hadn't planned that far ahead.

Catherine laughed again and pulled at his arm. "Come on, my big spender, I saw some for sale downtown. If we hurry, we can get the basics so it doesn't look like you have a tree growing out of your floor for no reason."

"Sounds good."

Catherine was smiling, happy, and it gave him hope. He reminded himself that for two people with a lot of walls, they'd made more progress than he'd expected them to. He bet that she likely felt the same way. After all, it was natural for them both to take a half step back every once in a while as they came up against their personal triggers, in the process of learning more about each other.

"Let's get a special ornament every Christmas," he suggested. "One that signifies something that happened that year."

"That's a nice idea," she said with a dreamy smile. "So maybe an ornament with a baby or one of a bride and groom?" Her cheeks pinked and he loved that she was feeling shy about their new little family, and shy about showing him that what they were building was something that she liked and wanted. She was brave and strong, but she also cared what he thought and wanted, too.

He pulled her loosely into his arms, giving her a light kiss.

"Maybe we'll need to get a few this year. Think there's one that says Our Family's First Christmas?"

She gave him a sideways look. "Does that mean we have to get one of those formal family pictures where we all wear the same color?"

"Most definitely." He grinned at her and she returned the smile before throwing back her glossy curls, her throat exposed as she laughed in his arms.

And in that moment he felt the connection again, and nothing in life had ever felt more wonderful.

———

CATHERINE AND ZACH had found a few ordinary glass ornaments in the hardware store and were now wandering Blueberry Springs, on the lookout for unique ornaments to mark their year. Xavier was in his stroller, the sidewalks having been cleared enough they could push it without too much difficulty.

Catherine wasn't impressed with how she'd allowed herself to revert back to a fearful state earlier in the day, and was relieved she and Zach had already found their way back to their normal selves. It felt right. Bigger and better than the doubts she'd had earlier about his break-in skills. This was Zach. Her Zach. Not some criminal working in the underworld and using his business as a leverage point for crime. She needed to keep her head on straight and quit letting her past rule her future.

"The florists might have something," Zach suggested, pointing the way. "They might even be having a Black Friday sale on ornaments."

They browsed through the shop, finding some pretty ornaments in the gift section, but not quite what they were looking for. Nevertheless, they came out with a few for their collection, and were continuing on their quest when they bumped into Logan.

"Did you get that last camera for Mandy's?" Logan asked Zach, and before long the two men were deep into the logistics of the final touches they wanted to put on the brownie factory's new security system. The talk was way over Catherine's head and she wandered on, window-shopping and figuring that Zach would catch up when he was done talking to Logan.

She came to a bridal shop with gorgeous fur-lined shawls and beautiful winter wedding gowns in the window. She spotted Ginger working inside and waved. The woman beckoned her in despite the Closed sign, and Catherine called over her shoulder to Zach, "Xavier and I will be in here."

The store's warmth enveloped her, and she realized she was slowly getting used to the mountain weather, enjoying the winter conditions and the cold. It wasn't as dark and dreary as London often was at this time of year, and she found she didn't miss its dampness and chill. Here, when it wasn't snowing, the skies tended to be bright, and there were days she needed sunglasses when she went out.

"I thought you were taking the day off?" Catherine asked. While they'd been choosing trees earlier, Catherine had understood that Ginger's store wasn't taking part in Black Friday with a big blowout sale, and that she'd given all her employees the day off.

"I am," Ginger assured her. "Sort of. Olivia wanted to tweak a dress, so I figured I'd come in, too, and take care of a few things." She pointed toward two women in an adjoining room. There was a small stage, with mirrors lining the walls in front of it. Windows that overlooked the street were covered with gorgeous floor-length curtains. A bride was standing on the stage, a curvy blonde in front of her pinning up the hem of her gown. The whole scene was like a dream.

Ginger's eyes were bright, her smile wide. "Logan and I live above the store, which enables me to have such bad work habits. I do love it though. There's nowhere else I'd rather be. So? Are you looking for a wedding dress? Is that why you're full of smiles?" The woman's eyes gleamed.

Catherine shook her head, but knew she *was* smiling. And it felt good. She could see herself with Zach, staying here with him long-term. Raising Xavier together like a real couple. Even being in love. It was still hard to believe that this man she'd met online was quickly becoming someone she thought of as a soulmate. Something wonderful sent to her after years of darkness. She'd thought she'd had a life back in London, but now she could see how closed off she'd been, how little she'd truly let people in.

"Zach and I are just looking for a bride-and-groom Christmas ornament for our tree," she told Ginger. "I thought maybe you'd have one?"

"I have a few things over by the register if you want to take a peek." She began leading Catherine over to a small display toward the back of the showroom. The store was amazing. Racks of dresses and accessories filled the space without it feeling crowded, and she longed to wander the aisles, feeling the different fabrics, dreaming of the different weddings that would fit each dress's style. The simple sheath on display to her left would call for a simple wedding, but elegant and sophisticated. The off-the-shoulder number beside it would work for something big and fun, with lots of kids running around and filling the dance floor.

"By the way," Ginger said, "Jill told me that if you drop your skillet and knives off she'll have them back from the sharpener guy in a few days. She'll get them back to you when they're done."

She led Catherine to the main counter, where a small tree by the cash register was sparsely covered with ornaments.

"I might have to check the back," Ginger said, eyeing her little display. "We had a bit of a run on these the other day."

Behind Ginger, screens were lit up with photos of brides. There were a few faces she recognized from around town, and she realized these weren't stock photos, but rather ones of real-life customers.

"You like the display?" Ginger asked, craning her neck to look behind her. "I was just updating some of the photos before you came in."

"They're beautiful." A picture of a dark-skinned flower girl flipped past, making her heart swell. Then one of a family all dressed in formal wear, arms around each other, followed by one of a bride and groom grinning at each other with so much love Catherine had to look away.

She would never have a reason to shop in a store like this and become immersed in the dream of happily ever after, where the dress was a representation of all that her life was—perfect and beautiful. Yes, things were great with Zach and she couldn't imagine them being better than they were, but a wedding? The two of them were already married. She was a mum. They hadn't married for the show. And just because there was a chance their marriage might become what most people hoped for, the wedding dream just didn't fit. They were having a reception, and there was no call for anything fancier than a semiformal dress. No gown. No veil. No hairdresser making her look like a goddess.

As Ginger hustled to the back to find what she swore was the perfect ornament, Catherine found herself drawn to a small display to the left of the counter. There were tiny tuxedos, meant for children Xavier's size. Adorable little bow ties and cummerbunds attached to the outfit.

Perfect for a wedding.

"Aren't those so adorable?" Ginger asked, returning with a small brown box.

Catherine nodded, unable to speak. She was stroking the fabric of a little suit jacket, and she realized her longing was probably obvious to the woman whose job it was to outfit women like her. Women who wanted a wedding.

She couldn't be that person.

"I know you and Zach are already married, and your reception is going to be fairly informal, but maybe you can find an excuse to put Xavier in one of those."

"Don't tempt me," Catherine said, forcing herself to release the outfit, not take it to the cash register. It was too easy to picture what her wedding would look like. The dresses, tuxedos, cake, flowers...everything.

She shook her head when she started imagining Xavier as a ring bearer. Her son couldn't even walk. Plus, there was the small fact that she was already married.

"Definitely create an excuse to have him wear a baby tux," the blonde who'd been working on the dress said as she joined them. The bride she'd been working with was in a changing room, switching back into her street clothes. "I'm Olivia Mattson, by the way."

"Catherine Tisdale," she as they shook hands, wondering how Olivia managed to look so beautiful and simply elegant in her jeans and sweater.

"Olivia designs wedding gowns," Ginger said.

"Married to Devon?" Catherine asked. "Thank you for the loan of the bassinet." She involuntarily found her gaze drifting to Olivia's midsection.

Olivia cupped her midriff with a hand and smiled. "You're welcome."

"She's going to need that back soon," Ginger said under her breath.

Olivia laughed. "Plenty of time, Ginger."

Ginger whirled, turning to face Catherine curiously, hands on her hips. "When was the last time you treated yourself?"

"Um?" She felt caught off guard, and even so, her heart sank as she thought over the question. Had she ever truly treated herself?

She couldn't afford to. And it didn't feel right to ask Zach to cough up money for something fancy like a beautiful wedding dress just because she thought it was a fun idea. Plus what if he said yes?

"We can work on Zach if he's the hang-up," Olivia said.

"I just..." She thought about photos of the celebration being posted on social media. A small, quiet gathering like what had been planned at Brew Babies next month was safe. But a real wedding reception would bring a significant security issue.

Safety first, she thought with a sigh. Always safety first.

Not the dream, but the reality.

That was what mattered. Not the beautiful dress and celebration.

Besides, they hadn't even reached the I-love-you stage of things. A big wedding didn't quite jibe with that fact.

"You don't want something larger than the wine and cheese at the pub?" Ginger asked. Her voice lifted at the end of her sentence, dangling that carrot in front of Catherine, just waiting for her to reach out to take a bite of the wedding dream so she could hook her and reel her in.

She was not getting hooked and reeled in.

Zach had already bowed out on the no-reception plan. She knew how easily it could become something big. Especially if she gave the women here the go-ahead to bully Zach into it—not that it would likely take much. He seemed to want whatever made her happy.

"I don't want photos and a big fuss. I just…" Her eyes drifted toward a gown with a beaded bodice. It had dream-dress potential. But sadly, it was way too fancy for anything she'd ever have, even if it would look absolutely amazing on her motherly curves.

"Then don't create a big fuss," Ginger coaxed. "Keep it simple. Get your guests to take photos and send them to you if you don't want to hire someone."

"I just don't want to be plastered all over everyone's social media." She added quickly, "It's silly, I know."

"Why not?" Ginger asked. "Are you shy about photos?"

Catherine shrugged.

"You're beautiful."

Olivia nodded in agreement. She was watching her thoughtfully, and Catherine worried what she might be figuring out about her.

"I get it," Olivia finally said, head tipped to the side, and Catherine panicked. "I used to be a model, and being out there and having everyone judging you is hard. Sometimes it's nice to lie low."

Catherine felt the stress flood out of her as quickly as it had come. She nodded, relieved she didn't have to tell them she believed she might have someone stalking her. "I don't like a lot of attention."

"Unless you're onstage," Ginger said. "I heard you really hammed it up with your hubby."

"There was hardly anyone in the room. Just Moe and Amy and that cowboy. Cole?"

"Oh, Cole. The man with the brooding soul. He's working through something. I bet the right woman could help with that," Ginger said with a quick smile.

"Set him up, set him up," Olivia chanted.

"I will. I will. I just need to figure out why he sits at the bar every afternoon with a shot of whiskey. If I can unlock that mystery I'll know who he needs."

"If the town wants to spoil you guys," Olivia said, changing the subject back to Catherine and a wedding, "let them. You've moved over here with hardly anything, and Zach is a bachelor. I doubt he even has a mixer. How are you going to do your Christmas baking?"

"He probably doesn't even have cookie sheets!" Ginger exclaimed. "You need to have as many parties as you can to load up on household stuff."

Catherine laughed. "His kitchen is fine."

"Oh, come on," Olivia said. "We want to dress you up. Please?"

"Lightly beaded bodice with an illusion back adorned with lace appliqués, and a flowing skirt," Ginger said. "Three-quarter-length sleeve."

That did sound amazing. She reminded herself that she was not going to try something on.

"That luscious cream in satin," Olivia said. She gave a gasp, leaning forward. "Chantilly lace overlay for the skirt."

The women fired more details back and forth,

building a look that Catherine could envision. One she wanted.

"Hair combs with pearls and crystals," Olivia said.

"Veil?" Ginger asked.

"Thin and long," Catherine blurted out. She could feel it flowing behind her on a breeze. She was getting into the dream, owning it. She could even imagine the way Zach would kiss her when they said their vows, the way Xavier would give them a gummy baby smile in his mini tuxedo.

She wanted it.

Badly.

"French twist," Olivia said definitively.

"With a few loose tendrils," Catherine said.

"Low heel," Ginger added.

"We don't have anything quite like this in stock, but I could definitely create it," Olivia said, her eyes twinkling with excitement.

"The reception is coming up fast," Ginger said.

"Wait!" Catherine held out a hand, eyes closed. Reception. That was all. "It's a simple gathering. People can come and go all evening. It's a wine and cheese. There's no need for a gown. It's just…it's not needed."

The smiles faded.

"Right," Ginger said, straightening her top. "I got carried away."

Olivia gave a sad smile and Catherine released a heart-wrenching sigh. There was no reason to spend a pile of money on a beautiful wedding just because she was enjoying kissing her husband. No reason at all.

ZACH WALKED into Ginger's shop, where the sheer estrogen of the store nearly knocked him sideways. Talk about Princessville. And yet the women were standing near the cash register looking deflated.

"What happened?" he asked. "Was there a celebrity divorce I should know about?"

"There's no excuse to build a dream dress for Catherine," Olivia explained. Ginger nodded, her face long.

"A wedding dress?" Zach asked carefully. Were they seriously moping about that? He watched Catherine out of the corner of his eye, curious whether this was attributing to her own less-than-happy look.

"We got caught up in the dream," Catherine said with a small laugh, shaking off the earlier mood. But there was a sadness in her eyes.

She wanted the dream.

The whole entire thing, from the ring to the

dress and cake, to the picket fence and happily ever after.

Ring.

He hadn't even gotten her a ring.

What kind of crappy husband was he? In fact, he wasn't even sure he had a copy of their wedding certificate.

That thought brought him up short. Shouldn't there be a paper trail? And shouldn't he have a copy of it? Or did Catherine have everything in her possession?

Ginger said something Zach didn't quite catch and he refocused on the women.

"You can wear a dress to the reception," he said to Catherine. Couldn't she?

"Not the one we dreamed up," Ginger said. "It's too amazing."

"Your wife would look so incredible," Olivia said. "We would have had to pick your dropped jaw up off the floor." She smiled as she sauntered past him to go talk to the woman who was exiting the fitting room. As Olivia moved by him, she tapped his chin to emphasize her point about the jaw-dropping factor of the dream dress.

What did this gown look like, anyway? He couldn't imagine Catherine being more beautiful than she already was, with her womanly curves and smooth skin. The idea that there could be more, that she wanted to stand up in front of friends and family and make all of this even more real than it already was, made him want to sign his name wherever needed.

Before Zach could decide where to start untangling this whole new wedding thing, Ginger waved a tiny tuxedo in front of him. "You need to get this for Xavier."

"I do?"

"You do." She set it by the cash register, Catherine's attention following the small garment.

"It's too formal," Catherine said weakly. The longing in her gaze was so strong it could have been bottled.

"He's a baby and is growing up so fast," Ginger said. "Nobody will think it's odd that he's in a tux. He'll be adorable. I say go for it."

"Are you pressuring her to purchase it?" Zach asked. Things were moving fast. Too fast. He needed to slow down and get a better lay of the land before deciding what the best option in this situation was.

"Such strong words," Ginger said.

"I know what you're doing," he said, adjusting Xavier's snowsuit so it was fully zipped up. Ginger was driving in the thin edge of a wedge. If they let her, they'd soon have a full-fledged wedding coming up, and he wasn't sure if that's what was wanted. He glanced at Catherine again.

He could see the conflicted feelings she was dealing with, the possibilities at war with each other.

Was a wedding what she wanted? Was she afraid to speak up for what she really preferred? If so, that was no way to handle a relationship.

"And what am I doing?" Ginger said sweetly, folding up the small black outfit.

Zach directed Catherine toward the door, pushing the stroller. "We'll talk to you later."

"But what about the tuxedo for Xavier?"

"We'll get it when we get our own attire."

Catherine's steps slowed and he gave a gentle nudge to her lower back. They needed to get out that door. They needed to talk, find a unified front that worked for both of them, or soon Blueberry Springs would be controlling their entire life. Or at least the wedding.

Wait. There wasn't supposed to be a wedding. Just a reception. Low-key. Simple.

He bet this was how the holidays got out of control for most people. You gave in on one small thing that didn't feel big at the time, and soon your quiet, at-home Christmas involved fifty relatives, three international flights and a credit card bill that would take months to pay off.

"I thought you were going to buy an ornament?" Ginger called after them, a pout clearly obvious in her voice. She was such a brat.

"Tomorrow," Zach promised, just before the door swung shut behind them. "Sorry," he said to Catherine. "Things looked like they were getting out of hand."

"We got caught up in...everything." She was shrugging off the conversation she'd had, the dream the women had helped her build, her cheeks pinker than the cold weather warranted.

"I thought you didn't want a big deal?" She hadn't even really wanted the reception. Well, she had, but she also hadn't. A wedding, though? It was a far cry from a casual get-together.

"I don't," she confirmed.

But she did, didn't she? So where was the truth? Somewhere in between?

"There's a fantasy you want, isn't there?" he insisted.

"I think most women dream about being a princess for a day." She was concentrating on the snowy sidewalk more than she needed to.

"Do you *want* a wedding?"

She inhaled as though about to speak, her lush mouth opening before she clamped it shut again. "I always dreamed I'd have one. But do I *want* one? I'm not sure."

They walked past a few more businesses, both of them lost in their thoughts.

"Do you want to have one with *me*?" Zach asked. He cleared his throat, wishing he felt confident.

"I can envision it, but it doesn't fit our reality." Her tone had a slight ring of amusement, almost as though she was slightly embarrassed to have been asked.

"What does fit our reality?"

"Honestly?" She stopped pushing the stroller, letting it come to a stop so she could face Zach.

"Honestly."

She looked so thoughtful Zach found himself wanting to move nearer, to lean in and catch every nuance of expression that flitted across her face.

"I'm not sure yet."

She was standing close enough that it could be perceived as an invitation. He accepted it, placing one hand on her waist, the other going to her hair. He bent his head like he was going to kiss her, and her lashes lowered as she anticipated contact.

"We have some time to figure things out," he whispered.

She tipped her head back slightly, her eyes opening, and he gave her a full kiss on the mouth, not caring if anyone passing by saw them. Her mittened hands were against his chest as she clung to his coat, and he wished there weren't so many layers of clothing between his flesh and hers. He wanted to feel her heat, feel the subtle shifts of her body against his as he kissed her back with longing.

He slowly pulled himself out of the kiss before things went too far.

Catherine watched him, her thoughts so heavy he could practically hear them speaking to him.

"What?" he asked gently.

"We got married online and have become friends. I don't know how this all fits."

He nodded, encouraging her to go on.

"We feel like a family." There was that bashful look again. "You've become like a boyfriend. I like that."

"So do I."

"I can see us becoming more than this, but I'm not sure…"

She was studying him with that gentle, open way of hers, and he wondered what she was searching for. What question she was trying to answer. He felt as though he should know, but he was lost in her eyes, the way the flecks of amber surrounding her irises were lined in black, like an island in a sea of blue.

He held her tight, not wanting her to slip away.

"We'll become more than this. This and other

things." He gazed at her, hoping she saw how steadfast he felt in his conviction. "But," he added gently, when he saw the fear flare up, "our relationship isn't ready for all of that. We have time and I'm not going anywhere." He slid his hands over hers. "However, we do have to figure out what kind of party we're having to celebrate our marriage."

"A wedding is over the top," she said, her expression one of warning, as though she expected him to say, "Let's do it!"

"I agree that right now it is, but I'm here for the long haul. I like you, Catherine. I don't see that changing. So if a wedding is what you want, maybe we go for it even though it feels like we're putting the cart before the horse that hasn't even been born yet."

She hugged him, pressing close.

"Let's keep it simple," she said.

"Are you sure that's what you want?"

"I already have what I want."

A warmth flowed through his chest as he realized that what she wanted was him.

Zach was a short way ahead of Catherine on the footpath leading to the lookout. Evergreens whispered on the left and right, and a jay optimistically followed his progress, hopping from branch to branch, hoping for a little treat. Zach had Xavier in the carrier snugged to his chest, and his heart was pounding hard from nerves. Parachuting into danger zones, avoiding poison and dodging bullets had led him to have sweaty palms in the past, but nothing like he had right now.

He had a plan, he reminded himself.

Stick to the plan.

Work the plan.

Modify the plan. Rework the plan.

Was that how it went? His training was failing him.

He had a ring in his pocket. He knew what he wanted to say. He could do this.

He'd caught Catherine searching Ginger's website instead of doing her accounting work the other afternoon. She'd had a wistful expression, her chin resting in her hand as she'd flipped through the online slideshow, before clicking over to a site with engagement and wedding bands.

Before she'd noticed him, he'd backed from the basement room and quietly retraced his steps to the main floor, before thundering down the stairs, giving her time to hide the sites before he appeared.

Catherine wanted the dream. The wedding. The ring. Everything.

And why shouldn't he give that to her?

He *would* give it to her.

But he would never again silently laugh at any jittery guy getting ready to propose.

The lookout over the town was just behind another curve up the trail. From the small clearing they could watch the sun set, the sky streaking pink and purple as lights flicked on across Blueberry Springs. He'd get down on one knee, Xavier strapped to his chest to show her that she could have both men in her life as her little family, and he'd say his speech about destiny and soulmates. She'd say yes. He'd light the torch he had in his backpack if they needed it, and they'd come back down the mountain as a true couple. Logan and Ginger would arrive in the parking lot with champagne to help them celebrate.

He knew this was what Catherine wanted, what she secretly wished for. So why was he such a bundle of nerves? They were already married. She'd already said yes.

But this time…this time she would be saying yes to a whole lot more. To the entire dream. To *him*.

He'd never felt like this about anyone, and he knew in some ways that his proposal was huge. It was akin to hoisting a huge neon sign that said Be Mine. I'm Going To Let You In And Love You."

Love you.

They hadn't even said those three words yet. Was he putting the cart before the unborn horse again? That did seem to be the way of their relationship, and so far it had worked for them.

Something snagged his senses, and he froze on the mountain path, instinctively putting a hand on the back of Xavier's head, while angling his body so it could serve as a shield to protect the child. He eased forward, the clearing slowly coming into view, where a man dressed in white camouflage gear waited.

Zach's free hand automatically went up, a silent signal to Catherine to halt. Her footfalls were steady, crunching on the snow behind him, her distant chatter about how fast he'd been walking cheery. She didn't stop, and he figured she hadn't come around the last corner yet.

The familiar man in front of him said nothing, simply held eye contact, his hands in the pockets of his heavy-duty pants.

"Whitman," Zach said.

An all-star agent for British intelligence. MI6. Their paths had crossed working on gang connections that extended across the globe, and Whitman was responsible for more arrests in the area of money laundering, murders, thefts and disappearances than any other agent he knew of. Zach could break his way into anything, but Simon Whitman could find a way to capture anyone.

But what was Simon Whitman doing in the mountains above Blueberry Springs outfitted in winter camo gear?

Simon.

Catherine's Simon?

No. Surely not.

The man gave a barely perceptible nod, as though he could see inside Zach's mind, watching him make the neural connections that helped him catch up with their story.

Zach nearly had to sit.

Agent Simon Whitman was Catherine's Simon. And that meant he was also Xavier's "deceased" father.

But he was very much alive.

CATHERINE BUMPED into Zach's back. She'd been feeling giddy with happiness as she followed him up the path. Zach had been acting with such tenderness over the past few days it had left her feeling as though she was on a permanent high. She knew they were simply in the I-can't-believe-how-lucky-I-am-to-have-discovered-you-and-nothing-can-go-wrong honeymoon phase of their relationship, but she was happy. Lighthearted and happy.

How could she not be? Her husband was not only carrying her heavy baby up the mountainside, but had suggested the whole excursion, not only to help her deal with the onset of yet more cabin fever, but to watch the sun set over the town.

Romantic!

So completely swoon-worthy.

Yes, she was happy. Giddy for the way this man was cherishing her and letting her into his life.

She was special.

His special someone.

"Is there a deer?" she asked, grabbing his coat after running into him. She glanced up and the hair on her neck prickled, sending shivers straight down her spine.

Something was wrong.

She peered around Zach's broad shoulder and felt as though her legs were about to give out under her.

Simon.

Simon was alive.

Alive!

No. It couldn't be him. She had to be seeing things. It *wasn't* him. It was someone else dressed all in white, like a snowy angel.

She squeezed her eyes shut, took a steadying breath, then reopened them. The man tipped his head, watching her in that way of his that told her he *was* real as well as very much alive.

How though? He'd died. There'd been a funeral. Had they buried an empty urn?

Why hadn't he told her he had survived the crash? Where had he been hiding? Why hadn't he taken her with him?

Her family hadn't run him off the road.

He hadn't died because he'd been a part of her life.

The rush of relief went as quickly as it had come as questions filled her mind. How had he found her? How had Simon, who was supposed to be dead, managed to head Zach and her off on a mountain path, with a look of determination and purpose in his solid gaze?

Fear coursed through her veins. If he'd found her...

She looked over her shoulder and edged closer to Zach.

"Simon?" Zach said, breaking the silence.

Zach knew Simon?

She took a step away from her husband, no longer certain about anything. The whole scene felt bizarre, totally illogical. But she couldn't escape, because Zach had Xavier. In fact, he'd insisted on carrying him. And now she was trapped, unable to run.

"Why are you here?" she asked Simon, finally finding her voice. "You—you died." She was shaking, her mind sprinting like a frightened jackrabbit, trying to find the exit, the answer. Anything that might save her.

"I couldn't tell you," Simon said, his tone even and emotionless.

She felt lightheaded and as though she might need to bend over, the full shock of seeing him sinking in.

Her baby's father was alive.

He'd been her boyfriend. A man she'd trusted. A man who might or might not have betrayed her family. They'd both been on the run for months, and the part of her that had feared he'd been killed by her family wanted to weep. He was alive.

But he'd left her pregnant, alone and on the run. And for what?

She swallowed hard, trying to slow her thoughts. Nothing made sense.

Beside her Zach shifted his weight, and her attention snapped to him. "Why do you know him?" she demanded.

"He's Xavier's father?" There was barely a question in the statement. Zach's eyes were unreadable. He'd closed himself off from her.

She focused on Simon whose gaze kept straying to her son. *Hers.* Not his, not theirs. He'd left her. Faked his death and abandoned her. He'd caused all this—the fear, the need to hide from the world, unable to trust anyone. Unable to figure out what had truly gone on, and how severe the threat to her and her son actually was.

"Why are you here?" Catherine stepped forward, ready to deck Simon for being so selfish. For failing to be honest, for hiding things from her.

"It wasn't safe to come sooner."

"And it's safe now?"

He didn't meet her eyes and her rage intensified.

"Were you the snitch?" He still didn't look at her. "Did you cause all of this? Did you put a target on my back?" His actions had threatened everything, hadn't they? And then, because he was either stupid or selfish, he'd burst into her new life and threatened everything once again.

"You need to leave." She pointed down the mountain even though he didn't look up to meet her fiery gaze. "Now. I never want to see you again."

What if she and Xavier weren't safe here?

Simon moved toward her, but Zach stepped between them, shielding her. "She's a civilian."

The man tipped his head, having one of those silent conversations she'd seen Zach and Logan have. "We need a minute," he finally stated, and Zach reluctantly eased to the side with an audible sigh.

"Make things right," he warned him.

"No." Catherine felt as though her eyes were daggers, slicing Simon, but he didn't seem to notice. "No," she repeated, this time to Zach. She was *not* talking to Simon. There was no way to make this right. She felt like crying at the futility of it all. To have come so far, to have built so much with this man, only to have to leave it all behind once again.

Zach's shoulders drooped as he said, "It's probably for the best if you hear him out."

"No."

"I'll be just down the path if you need me." When he met her gaze, there was nothing there. Just a wall. He was shutting her out, shifting aside instead of stepping up and claiming his spot beside her, and it hurt worse than it had losing Simon. As Zach shuffled down the path, he moved as though a part of him had broken.

She longed to reach out to him, but he was a part of this somehow, and she felt as though she could no longer trust him—the only person she'd ever felt she could.

"I don't have much time, Patty," Simon said, leading her to the clearing.

"I'm no longer Patty."

He still had that same rugged look, that serious, thoughtful expression and that way of gazing at her that made her feel as though she was seen by him. It was similar to Zach's. Only Zach made her feel like he cared, while Simon? She swallowed hard as the truth sank in. He wasn't here for her. He was here for himself. He needed something, and whatever it was, she was determined not to give it to him.

"I'm married," she stated.

"I wanted to give you this." He held out an envelope. It was thick. Thick with payoff. "For Xavier."

She crossed her arms across her chest so she wouldn't automatically take it as he pressed the envelope closer. She wasn't taking his bribe. Taking his money would be accepting the way he'd taken her life and thrown it away. "How do you know Xavier's name?"

Simon glanced down the sloping trail, and Catherine followed his gaze to where Zach was pacing, just out of earshot. He kept one hand on Xavier's back as though afraid the boy would vanish if he didn't touch him. Simon finally looked at her, his expression pained.

"How do you know Zach?" she asked. "Did he tell you where to find me?"

"Zach will keep you safe."

"What do you mean?" The grim set of Simon's jaw told her there was danger lurking. He'd stirred a pot and now she had to pay the price. "Do they know where I am? Is someone looking for me?"

"Zach's an associate—a retired one. He understands."

"Understands what?" Her stomach was threatening to drop out, as well as her heart. The world was spinning as things clicked into place, forming puzzle pieces she wanted to deny.

Zach was an associate?

Simon's envelope of cash. A payoff for being involved with him. But the worst part was that Simon had said Zach understood.

Understood Simon. Understood how to break and enter. How to keep things hush-hush.

He had secrets. A past.

Zach had said no thief would dare mess with his home.

Now she knew why.

He was just like her father.

She'd found him because Leo, also a friend of Simon's, had recommended she come here.

And she'd been naïve enough to listen. To trust him.

Simon was an associate, Zach was an associate.

No matter how hard and how far she ran, she'd never escape her family's reach. She would be on the run for the rest of her life.

She staggered toward the lookout bench as her legs lost their strength.

But instead of Simon catching her, Zach did, her son still strapped to his chest. When she looked up into Zach's eyes, she knew what she saw was real. But she'd thought she'd seen that in Simon's eyes, too, once upon a time.

And Simon had played her. He'd put her life and Xavier's in danger.

She shook off Zach's grip on her arm, vowing that this time when she ran nobody was going to find her.

Nobody.

ZACH WASN'T sure what Simon had said to Catherine, but he knew it couldn't have been good.

His wife shook off his touch, jerking the carrier clips that had Xavier strapped to him. Within seconds, the small child was clipped to her instead, his words falling on deaf ears as she mindlessly turned to flee.

"What did you say?" Zach growled at Simon as Catherine fled down the mountain path.

He couldn't believe the agent was Xavier's father. That he'd left her to figure this all out on her own. There was the idea of civilian casualties, and then there was this betrayal that had her and her child unprotected and on the run. He wanted to string the man up by his toenails.

Simon shook his head, face averted. "Classified. Go to her. Keep her here, keep her hidden, keep her safe."

Zach clenched and unclenched his fists, his chest was cold without Xavier snuggled against him, cold without Catherine's trust. He feared he might never get her back.

"For the record, I hope you rot in hell," he said to Simon as he turned to run after Catherine.

He caught up with her partway to the parking lot, the engagement ring safe in his pocket. How had everything gone so wrong so quickly?

"Catherine, wait," he said, jogging up behind her. He struggled to use a calm and soothing voice that would settle her, instead of the panicked one that threatened to burst forth at the idea of losing her.

What had Simon gotten her involved in? Was he the stalker she was trying to hide from? Or was it worse? Much, much worse?

Her jaw was set and she'd thrown up that wall he'd worked so hard to scale. He could practically see her securing every padlock at her disposal to shut him out.

Helpless, he followed her down the trail, pleading with her. Her boots slipped on the packed snow as she hurried to get ahead of him, and he feared she'd fall and hurt herself and Xavier. He dropped back despite wanting to strong-arm her into listening to him. Moments later she burst into the parking lot, and Zach slowed once again as he caught sight of Logan reaching out to her.

He could hear his friend's deep voice saying, "Hey there, my sheila, what's up?"

She bolted in the opposite direction.

Zach picked up his pace, fearing she was about to disappear no matter what the risk might be.

CATHERINE TORE ACROSS A SNOWY MEADOW, lungs and legs screaming for her to slow down, wishing the packed path she was on went straighter so she could get to the house faster. Get the diaper bag and disappear.

Forever.

Why had she left it at home? How had she become so complacent so quickly that the diaper bag was just one more thing to carry, and she no longer felt the need to bring it everywhere if she could get away with simply bringing an extra diaper? It wasn't about the diapers!

Xavier was fussing at the rough treatment he was receiving as he bounced in the front carrier. She pressed her hand against his back, supporting his head and holding him close, but continued to run as though someone was after her.

She darted a glance over her shoulder, but nobody was there. Not Zach, not Simon, not Logan. She slowed her pace so she wouldn't twist an ankle, but kept moving toward town, the warm little houses with their puffs of wood smoke and furnace exhaust creating clouds above them. It might appear idyllic and safe, but she no longer felt that.

Simon hadn't died, but had been tracking her. Had come to pay her off, possibly leading someone else right to her in the process. There was nobody she could trust.

She had been living with a man who was associated with the family she'd tried to escape.

She'd been trying so hard to lead a different life that she hadn't even seen what was right in front of her. Again.

She reached the house, surprised and relieved to find Zach wasn't already there waiting for her.

He wouldn't be long.

She needed to hurry.

"WHAT DID YOU SAY TO HER?" Logan asked. There was a hint of lighthearted amusement in his tone, but his eyes told Zach he was well aware that something serious had happened on the mountainside.

"Why was Simon Whitman up there?" Zach demanded.

"Simon?"

"Who's Simon?" Ginger asked, coming around the car, her brow furrowed. "What happened with Catherine?"

Without looking, Logan held up the car keys for Ginger to take. He said to her, "It's time for you to head home and stay there until I say otherwise."

Ginger's mouth opened to protest, but instead she took the keys, her confusion turning to concern as she said, "I love you. Be safe, okay?"

Logan turned briefly to Ginger, placing a kiss tight against her lips before releasing her, his attention back on Zach as Ginger started the car, pulling away.

"What did Whitman want?" Logan asked.

Zach's chest hurt like someone had knifed him. "He's Xavier's father."

Logan's expression turned thoughtful.

"We need her history," Zach said. "All of it. Who's she hiding from? How is Whitman involved? Why did he leave her unprotected and on the run?"

He wanted to hit something. Hard. Rage was ripping through him with the force of a category five hurricane, tearing away his resolve to simply be an average citizen. He needed to act. Needed to pull favors. Needed to dig to the bottom of this and get Catherine to safety.

Something was very, very wrong.

"I thought you wanted to see if you could handle normal life," Logan said carefully.

"That was before an active M16 agent crashed my marriage proposal, in the middle of nowhere." Zach froze for a second as things clicked into place.

He swore under his breath.

Simon Whitman was the one responsible for taking down the Davies gang in the UK.

"See if Catherine's real name is Patty Davies. And find out which nightclub she used to work in." He'd bet anything it was the one Simon had infiltrated when he'd gone undercover to make his arrests. Had he used her to gain insider information on her family? Was she an active part of the crime family? She'd said she was alone by choice. Was the choice face prison, or run away and assume a new identity in a foreign country?

Had he been harboring a fugitive?

Although if Catherine was in fact Patty, journalists covering the story believed she'd been trying to escape the family for some time. She'd told Zach she'd unwittingly helped commit a crime at the nightclub. Her shame and agony over having a hand in the money laundering had been genuine.

His best bet was that Simon had used her, then faked his own death to give himself a way out, leaving Catherine with no choice but to flee.

Whitman hadn't taken care of her. He'd put her in danger. But what was the specific danger? Her own family? Were they blaming her for ending their empire and putting them behind bars?

She *was* Patty Davies, wasn't she? She was the missing woman on the news that he'd worried may have been a casualty in the massive takedown. She was alive and had been living with *him*. And he hadn't even made the connection.

Zach hated that he'd missed that. But even more, that Simon Whitman might have just painted a new target on his wife and child.

"Find out where Jerry Davies is," Zach said, dread creeping in. Missing these things had lost them time. Time they needed to stay ahead of what was coming.

"He escaped jail," Logan replied.

"I know," Zach said grimly. "And I fear he might be looking for payback."

XAVIER WAS HOWLING in his carrier as Catherine grabbed the car seat from its spot at the door, along with the diaper bag. Two more steps and she'd be gone. The front door opened and she braced herself for the upcoming confrontation with Zach as well as his well-earned confusion.

She would lie. She would tell him things weren't working out.

But it wasn't Zach.

She dropped the seat and bag, backing up so quickly she nearly tripped.

It was her cousin Jerry, the escaped convict. The man the family had jokingly nicknamed Bucket. And the reason for that was the only thing she could focus on.

He was here to end her, because he believed she was responsible for how he'd been thrown in jail, along with the rest of the family.

"Please," Catherine said, her voice so weak and helpless sounding, even to her own ears, that it decimated her limited confidence. She bounced gently, trying to calm Xavier, who was still upset. "It wasn't me."

"I saw you talking to him," Bucket said, jutting out his chin, his British accent clipped with displeasure.

"Who?"

Her cousin stepped closer, arm raised, ready to strike her.

"Please! The baby," she begged, cowering and wishing she was stronger. She edged back, thinking if she could get to the umbrella stand she might manage to take a swing at Jerry with Zach's baseball bat.

281

"Don't play dumb," he said. He flipped back his jacket to reveal a holster that kept a handgun nestled against his side.

"I moved out from home at age sixteen, and haven't been back except for my mum's funeral. You know that." Xavier was kicking and wriggling, about to cause a big fuss again, and she feared how Bucket might react to the noise.

"Whitman was the manager. You two were close enough to have a baby. I know you helped him. I know you told him things nobody else could know."

Simon. She'd told him so little, but she knew Bucket wouldn't care. He'd pulled out his gun and clicked off the safety.

"You let in a rat. *You* are a rat."

Catherine eased back another step. She had two choices. Grab for the bat, or keep backing down the hall and through the kitchen, where she might be able to turn and race out the rear door. Or loop around through the dining area, then the living room and out the front, not allowing herself to get trapped. The problem was she wasn't going to be faster. Not carrying Xavier. She was going to have to be smarter.

"I told him nothing. I *know* nothing."

"You told him everything," Jerry growled.

"I didn't. I swear!" Sometimes he'd ask her

weird questions that puzzled her, but she'd never said anything that could have led to him putting her entire family behind bars. "I've spent my life trying to get away from you guys. My entire life!"

Bucket's tone was suddenly calm, resolved. "Patty, you know too much."

Catherine stumbled past the umbrella stand. She couldn't swing the bat. Not hard enough. Not with Xavier strapped to her chest.

"Why would I want my family in jail?" With fear hammering in her chest she stepped forward, finger pointed his way in accusation. "Maybe it was you. Maybe *you* would benefit from everyone in jail."

"With myself in the slammer? Don't be daft."

"You don't look like you're in jail at the moment, do you? Maybe this was all part of *your* big plan. You were always looking for ways to screw people over. Maybe you wanted everyone in jail so you could rule the gang."

"Nobody leaves the family! The family comes first!" He was angry now, the butt of his gun smashing a hole in the wall as he swung his arm in the narrow hallway.

Xavier was crying, and Catherine hoped that this time their neighbor George would go straight to the police instead of calling Zach to complain about the noise.

"How did you find me?" she asked, trying to keep Jerry talking. "Social media? Facial recognition? Simon? Leo? Zach?" If she got out of here she needed to know how to be smarter next time.

"I followed a little bird." He was stroking his gun in a way that made her very nervous.

Never trust anyone. Ever.

There was a knock at the front door, and in Bucket's split second of hesitation, Catherine called out, "Come in!"

As the door swung open she realized that if it was George, she was doomed. In fact, anyone who would bother to knock wouldn't be somebody who could help her, but someone she'd be bringing in to what could quickly become a deadly mess.

Jerry grabbed Catherine's arm, squeezing so hard she knew she'd have bruises. A moment later she felt the unrelenting pressure of his gun pressed to her back.

"Hey," Jill said smoothly, coming into the room after kicking off her large boots. "I brought that stuff back. Your final bill was only twenty bucks! I think he liked Ginger's story about the bride who got stuck in her dress and so he gave us all an extra discount." Jill had the box of sharpened knives and the cast-iron skillet in her arms, and she slowed as she caught sight of Jerry.

"This really isn't a good time," he said coldly.

"Oh, I can see that," she said easily, picking up speed as she glided farther into the house, practically herding them on down the hall and into the sunny kitchen. "But I really must drop this off or I'll forget. You know how it is."

"I said—"

"Enough out of you," Jill said, flashing him a look. Catherine silently tried to convey to Jill that she needed to leave. Now. And somehow take Xavier with her.

"You should check out your pan. It looks brand-new," Jill said. She was right in front of her now, her eyes locked on Catherine's.

Jill shook the box, and dutifully, Catherine reached into it, closing her eyes as she feared Jerry's reaction. She retrieved the cast-iron skillet and the gun pressed harder. The newly sharpened knives were in the bottom, but she didn't dare take one, knowing that it could easily be turned on her, injuring herself or the child strapped to her torso.

She held the pan. It was heavy. Impossible to wield with authority, especially with a gun pressed against her spine.

"Just like new," Jill said calmly.

"It's time for you to leave," Jerry said.

Jill quickly reached into the box at the same time that she dropped it, her hands suddenly full of long blades. "Sweetie, I think we're just getting started."

Catherine felt as though she was going to faint. Her friend had brought knives into a gunfight.

The gun's pressure left Catherine's back as Jerry tightened his grip on her. Xavier was quiet while the world seemed to shift, and then a loud crack filled the room and plaster rained down over them as Jerry shot a hole in the ceiling. Catherine jumped, her heart pumping hard as her baby startled and let out a shriek.

Jerry was still behind her, but now the gun was aimed at Jill instead of Catherine. Jill held one of the knives by its blade, the handle extended toward the man. Her gaze was steady, as was her breathing. "Did I tell you my father owns the gun range in town, Catherine? I think I did. I used to compete as a sharpshooter. I'll have to show you my trophy case one day. I also learned some knife fighting along the way. I'm deadly accurate."

There was a fierceness in her friend's unwavering gaze, and for a moment Catherine thought they might just find a way to come out of this alive.

14

When Zach saw where Catherine was going—taking the footpath back to town—he hopped into his Land Rover, not at all surprised when Logan took the passenger seat. And not just because his wife had taken his vehicle back to town already.

"You going to tell me everything?" Zach asked, his jaw so tight his words were barely understandable. If Logan was in the vehicle and not already digging up the requested info on Catherine's background, it meant his friend knew more than he'd been sharing.

Logan grunted, then said, "After Simon Whitman faked his death, he had undercover agent Leo Barrellies, who had been acting as a bartender and friend to Catherine, contact her and tell her to go into hiding. Simon had prearranged pinch points that would push her here."

"No," Zach shook his head. "That doesn't add up." If it was true, then he had been played. He'd had to sign into that dating and marriage site and invite her here. He'd had to... Wait. All those things about their wooing that he didn't recall... He'd assumed he'd had too many whiskeys to remember, but what if he hadn't? What if it hadn't been him chatting with her online?

He paused for a second before asking Logan, "What's your involvement?"

"I was contacted shortly after she arrived, to keep an eye on things."

"An eye on me?" If Zach hadn't been driving he would have grabbed Logan by his collar and forced him to spill everything he knew about Catherine—his *wife*—and had been keeping from him, his best friend.

"On her situation."

"Why wasn't I told?"

Logan drew in a long breath.

"Tell me the truth." Logan hesitated and Zach added, "I was used by MI6 and maybe others. She's my wife."

"Technically, an online marriage—"

"She's my *wife*," Zach repeated forcefully. "And if the courts don't see that, then we will get married again. Do you understand me? This is my family we're talking about." He slammed the steering wheel, causing the vehicle to swerve.

"I get it," Logan said quickly. "I get what it's like to have the woman you love threatened or in a dangerous situation."

The woman you love.

Zach loved her, didn't he? Really and truly, honest to goodness.

"I tried to make sure none of this involved you so you could have a real chance with her. A chance where you wouldn't be doubting her intentions or turning into an agent."

"I need to know what we're dealing with." Zach took a corner too quickly, sending a fluffy gray cat scurrying across the street and into the square on Main Street.

"The Catherine you know is the missing daughter of the Davies gang. Her real name is Patty Davies," Logan said, a hint of guilt in voice. "Records show she's never been involved in the family activities."

Thank goodness for that. Zach wasn't sure how he'd feel if he discovered he'd fallen for a criminal.

Logan quickly filled him in on Catherine's past, explaining how she'd left home at a young age, avoiding her family until the sting operation exposed that she had been working in their nightclub, which had been a front for a massive money-laundering scheme. Logan spoke without emotion, as though reading from a report. He had switched into agent mode, shutting off any feelings or personal affiliations. It was time for Zach to do the same. Although this time it might be difficult.

"She didn't know she was working for her family?" Zach confirmed.

"Correct."

How could she not know?

Then again, it had taken a lot of failed operations and missing operatives to bring the family to justice. They might just be that good.

Zach sped through Blueberry Springs, the small town never feeling so large. Catherine had been able to take the footbridge over the river, a shortcut that would get her home before him even though he had the advantage of speed.

Logan continued, "Simon Whitman was sent to get close to her, to gain her trust. He'd originally assumed her to be involved, since she was booking headliners, bringing in a stream of cash that gave the club room to fudge their books without causing suspicion. It took months for him to get close enough to discover that she was oblivious to what was happening in the back rooms."

Zach grew hot under the collar, thinking what all Simon had done to get close enough to

Catherine to gain her trust, as well as to get her pregnant.

"He needed to influence her into making certain bookings, so he could set up the gang and get the evidence he needed in order to put them away," Logan said gently, no doubt sensing Zach's rage.

"He used her."

"You know how this job is."

"He got her pregnant!"

Logan's jaw flexed, but he said calmly, "Sometimes you have to do whatever it takes to get close to someone."

"It was unethical to ditch her like that."

"Condoms break. Accidents happen."

"Xavier isn't an accident." Zach couldn't imagine Catherine without her son.

"You know what I mean. A single mom is small collateral for putting these men away. We're talking missing people, Zach. Murders. Drug trafficking. Lives being ruined. You hear me?"

"He put *her* life in danger."

"The man was doing his job. He sent her here, to protect her while maintaining his cover as a dead man. There was no way he could show his face, or he'd be in the morgue. These guys don't forgive and forget." His tone softened. "We've all had to make impossible choices, Zach. Get your heart out of this."

"I don't want to," Zach muttered stubbornly. He hated the greater good right now. He truly did. "Why did Whitman come here? What's going on?"

"I don't know."

"He offered her an envelope."

"The mission ended with the convictions." After a long moment, he added, "Child support?"

"She didn't take it." She must hate Simon. Hate what he did to her and her family. Assuming she even knew.

"Does she know that Simon's MI6?"

"He said he didn't break cover. It's likely she still thinks he's a normal guy who got too close, got too greedy, and when the heat cranked up, turned tail and ratted out everyone. He's the no-good boyfriend who faked his own death when the heat got to him and left her behind."

"I can't believe he didn't get her put into protection."

She had to hate the man. Even with his background, knowledge and understanding, Zach despised Simon.

He cringed as he asked, "Does she know I used to be an agent?"

"I don't think so. Ginger said she's been careful not to let it slip."

As Zach slammed the vehicle into Park outside

his home, he asked, "Why did Simon send her to me?"

"Because he wanted to keep her safe."

THEY WERE AT A STANDOFF. Jill looked ready to throw the knife into Jerry's throat. And he looked ready to pull the trigger and send a bullet through hers. Jerry's grip was still tight on Catherine's arm and she was caught in the middle, Xavier hiccupping and squirming at being ignored in his state of distress. Tears streaked down Catherine's face as she waited for the standoff to end.

There wasn't even a tremble in Jill's hand, and Catherine noticed she had an odd tattoo shaped like an apostrophe on the inside of her wrist. The fact that she was noting tiny details caused Catherine to wonder if these were her last moments. If this was the beginning of the reel where her life flashed before her eyes.

More tears slid down her cheeks as she realized all the things she would miss. Seeing Xavier grow up. Getting to know Zach better.

No, that she wouldn't miss. He was as rotten as the man holding her hostage. An *associate*. Bile rose up in her throat at the thought. How had she missed that in both Simon and Zach? Simon, who'd left her high, dry, pregnant and in danger, so he could save himself. Zach, his associate. Who'd made her think he loved her so she would stay. Here where she could be found.

She'd fallen for a criminal.

She'd tried to turn over a new leaf and be someone else, but it hadn't worked out. She could never be that wonderful, innocent person because that simply wasn't her life.

But it could still be Jill's.

Catherine twisted in Bucket's grip, putting an arm in front of her new friend to protect her, securely placing herself in the middle.

"Just shoot me. I'm tired of running. I'm tired of being betrayed. I'm tired of people not being who they say they are. And I'm tired of being lied to."

"My pleasure," Bucket said with a wicked smile, swinging the gun a few inches so it lined up with her instead of Jill. Catherine was still holding the skillet, and she raised it in front of Xavier, hoping it could somehow spare him from what would surely be a brutal close-range shot.

But before she could shut her eyes and brace for the inevitable, Jill stepped back, cocking her arm. Her wrist flicked forward in one fluid move, releasing the knife through the air as the gun went off. Catherine jumped, the skillet jerking as though of its own volition. She hadn't protected Xavier! She'd flinched!

Jill stumbled, knocking into Catherine and her wailing child. Jerry was bleeding, cursing. He'd released Catherine and she spun, scanning for the best route out of the house. She needed the diaper bag.

Shouts filled her ringing ears as Zach and Logan entered the kitchen, guns drawn.

"Put down your weapon, Jerry!" Zach shouted. The walls spit and exploded behind the men as Bucket began firing off rounds.

Catherine dropped to her hands and knees, Zach's African violet landing in front of her, dirt spilling as its pot shattered. Behind her, Zach lunged across the room like a bull toward a matador's cape, sending Bucket into the wall with a sickening crunch. As Catherine crawled toward the hall to the front of the house, awkwardly cradling Xavier so he didn't bounce around in his front carrier, she spotted Zach lifting her cousin to the ceiling, then slamming him down on the kitchen floor.

Gasping for air, Catherine scrambled to her feet among Xavier's shrieks. Jill stumbled into her, half pushing, half helping her as they fled to the front door.

"Go, go, go!" Jill kept saying.

Catherine reached down on her way out of the

house to snatch the handle of the diaper bag. Hitting the front walk at a dead run, she heard George hollering from his step about the gunshots bothering his dog and how he was calling the police.

Adrenaline fueled her legs as she skittered down the road, directionless. Hooking the diaper bag handle over her arm, she checked Xavier and her hands for signs of blood, but didn't see any.

"This way!" Jill slid and slipped around an icy corner of the sidewalk in her stocking feet. "This way."

Catherine followed, running until she couldn't any longer, her breathing so labored she thought her lungs would implode. With a hand on her arm, Jill kept pushing her forward, then into an open garage and on inside the attached home.

From the living room carpet, where he was stretched out, playing with his daughter, Devon Matson looked up in surprise.

"We're not here," Jill told him.

"Okay," Devon said carefully. He got up, easing toward Catherine. "I've seen the movie *Tangled*. I know what a woman can do with a skillet."

Catherine's breath was coming out in a whistle, a terrified-animal sound. She didn't want to stop moving, but her legs were burning, her lungs in pain.

"Maybe I should take this," Devon said. He

gently pulled the heavy cast-iron object from her fingers. Her whole arm ached from its weight and the intensity of her grip. She should have dropped the thing, as it had no doubt slowed her down. "That's an interesting mark." He touched a deep, shiny scratch along its bottom.

"She stopped a bullet with it," Jill said. Her own hands were pressed to her knees and she was trembling. "She saved my life." Jill straightened, swinging her arm as if holding the skillet, echoing the move Catherine had instinctively made when Bucket had squeezed the trigger.

She'd almost gotten Jill shot. She couldn't stay here. She couldn't put these innocent people at risk.

Catherine took a step back, deciding which door to use. The back. "I need to go."

"No." Devon grasped her shoulders. "You're here. You're safe."

Little Abigail was toddling around the coffee table, chatting happily.

Catherine had put the girl in danger, as well as Xavier. Moments ago she'd stepped forward and asked to be shot. What had she been thinking?

"They may have seen us come here," she said. "I have to leave!"

"Who?" Devon asked.

"I have a feeling they're pretty busy at the moment," Jill said.

An image of Zach slamming her cousin onto the floor, as if he'd made such moves before, shook her to the core. He'd called Jerry by name. How did Zach know all these people? She felt as though she was on the verge of hysteria, her perfect dream morphing into a nightmare.

"I need to leave."

Devon kept an eye on her as he lifted his phone to his ear. Moments later he said, "Scott? We have a situation. Call Zach and Logan."

Catherine was shaking her head. "No. No." Her instinct was telling her to run. Run and never stop.

Devon set down his phone and nudged her over to the couch. "Jill, close the curtains, please." He made Catherine sit. With tense muscles, she clutched the diaper bag and Xavier who was still strapped to her. "Just breathe. You're safe here. Scott is coming."

No. She shook her head.

She couldn't trust anyone.

When flickers of flashing blue and red lights made their way through the front curtains, she saw her opportunity to flee and took it.

ZACH WAS at Devon's back door, waiting.

His cheek was throbbing from where Jerry had managed to land a hit. It wasn't the first time he'd fought the man, but this time he'd been prepared, and had definitely come out on top. Between himself and Logan, the gangster had been cuffed and ready for Scott in mere seconds.

By then Catherine, Xavier and Jill had fled. Which was probably good. He hadn't wanted Catherine or Xavier to see him pounding the crap out of one of their relatives. He'd had to act fiercely and quickly so he didn't add to the deep scars Jerry had left the last time he'd underestimated the man.

Zach angled himself so he couldn't be seen by anyone exiting the back door as Scott pulled up out front of Devon's place.

Sure enough, the second the front door opened and Scott stepped in, Catherine was out the back.

Trust nobody.

"Need a ride?" he asked, as she approached the steps that led off the back deck.

Catherine came to a sudden stop, backing against the wall by the door, her hands splayed against its surface.

She was afraid of him.

"Jerry's in custody. You're safe."

"He doesn't work alone." She was shivering, and

Zach wasn't sure if it was from shock, the cold or fear.

"Let's get you inside," he said, taking a step closer. It was cold enough that she could get frostbite, her nose already red from the wind.

"I'm not going anywhere with you," she said quickly.

"That's fine." He eased back, hands out in front so she could see that he was unarmed.

"I trusted you."

"And I trusted *you*," he replied, feeling a sting of anger for how she'd kept all this from him, how he'd overlooked the signs.

"I didn't do anything to you," she said.

"I didn't do anything to you, either."

"You told them I was here. You were holding me for them." She was blinking rapidly, twitching. "You lied to me."

"No." He shook his head. "No, I'm out of the game, Catherine. I'm not involved. I just want to keep you safe. That's why they sent you here, and that's all I want to do."

"No. You're with them."

"Catherine…" It was time to reveal his identity, but he never had before and the story stuck in his throat.

"I'm not like my family." She was sobbing now, broken. "Just let me go."

"I used to work with Simon, but I don't any longer. I've retired."

"I don't care! I don't date criminals."

"No, you date agents," he said calmly. "Simon is MI6. Myself? I was with an elite international agency. So was Logan. Simon came to the nightclub because he was working undercover. Same with Leo."

Catherine was watching him out of the corner of her eye. "I don't believe you." But there was a wariness in her voice, as if she might want to believe. She just wouldn't let herself.

"Why did Simon come here today?" he asked.

"It's none of your business."

"It is if I'm going to keep you safe."

"That's not your job."

"He's an active agent. It was a risk, coming to talk to you. He can't be involved in your life, Catherine."

"I let you in. I let Simon in. And look what happened! Just look!"

"I can keep you safe."

"No," she said, shaking her head. "I can't keep *you* safe. I can't keep anyone safe."

"That's not your job. I'm trained for this."

Her eyes squeezed shut, like she was trying to block out a memory or thought. "Jill almost got shot. Because of me. Simon got run off the road.

What if Xavier..." She shook her head again and, with a sharp breath in, closed her eyes.

"Catherine, I love you."

She opened them again, those beautiful, pain-filled blue eyes. "This isn't real. We don't know each other. Not our true selves."

"It *is* real. I know you. I know your heart. I fell for Catherine, not Patty. I love Catherine's honesty and kindness. She is a good woman."

"She isn't real."

"She is to me."

Catherine stared at him as though wanting to believe. Then she ran past him, and Zach tipped his face to the gloomy gray sky, forcing himself to let her go.

ZACH STOOD outside the hallway that led to the jail cell in the Blueberry Springs police station. Lately it seemed it was getting a lot of use.

"Logan," Zach said quietly, calling the man over.

"What's up?"

"The Rochester gang. Is that cover still active?"

Logan narrowed his eyes. A few years back several agents had created a pretend gang as a cover. It was secretive and deadly, taking credit for acts of terrorism and abuse, building an air of mystery around it that made most criminals uneasy.

"With assistance from the press, agents have been maintaining the story."

Alive and well. Zach now had a cover he could step into.

Logan warned, "You're no longer an active agent."

"I'm just going to speak his language in there." He jabbed a thumb in the direction of the jail cell.

"I hear that being court-martialed is worse than a month of solitary surveillance."

"Trust me. It's fine."

"Trust has nothing to do with this."

"I'm not asking you to participate."

Logan sighed. "You know I have your back, but I deny all knowledge of whatever you're about to do."

"That's fine." Zach flagged down Scott. "Can I have a moment with the perp, please?"

"So polite," Logan muttered under his breath, as Scott moved toward the holding cell. "You saying 'please' should be a tip-off that you're up to no good."

"A man can be polite and still have good intentions," Zach replied.

"Not if his name is Zach Forrester." Logan slipped into the room that would allow him to watch Zach through a two-way mirror. He caught the door before it closed, saying, "Do you need a babysitter in there?"

"I've got this." Zach cracked his knuckles, mentally planning his approach.

"If I'm court-martialed, I know nothing. You're on your own."

"Fair enough."

Zach let himself into the interrogation room, noting how they were always the same. He could be in Tel Aviv or New York. Heck, he could be at the South Pole and he wouldn't be able to tell the difference from inside this room.

Jerry was led in, his hands and ankles shackled together. Scott cuffed him to the table, which was bolted to the floor in the middle of the room. There was no need, but Zach supposed the small-town officer wasn't used to the stuff he was. Scott probably dealt more with people pulling U-turns in the middle of Main Street than with international criminals.

"You a cop now?" Jerry asked. He had a bruise under his eye, courtesy of Zach, and a red-stained bandage wrapped around his forehead, courtesy of Jill and her knife throwing skills. "Because you still fight dirty."

Zach said nothing, simply spun the metal chair

around so its back was facing Jerry's side of the table, then straddled it.

"I'm still with Rochester."

"You were never with them. You're a cop."

"Here's how this is going to go…" Zach said smoothly.

"You don't get to tell me squat. Just send me back across the pond."

"And that's where I think we should deal with this. On your home turf."

Jerry stilled, eyes narrowing.

"Let me lay it out for you. If you ever even think of touching Patty, your pretty girlfriend, Tricia, is gone. And that little boy you think nobody knows about over in Ireland? He's gone, too."

Jerry awkwardly lurched to his feet, his chains rattling and restricting him. "You don't get to threaten me."

"Patty's with me. You even look at her, Rochester comes after you. It's that simple." Zach was calm, his anger giving his voice a hard, almost lethal tone that had Jerry resizing him.

"You're not with them," the man said, his voice a tad too high. He was sweating, dampness forming at the edge of his hairline.

"I'm worse than just with them." Zach leaned forward, lowering his voice as he stared at Jerry. He gave that a moment to sink in. When Jerry's

Adam's apple bobbed, Zach added, "Like I was saying, if you or any of your family or associates come near Patty ever again—and I will know if you do— we'll empty that secret bank account."

"It's no secret. Everybody has one of those. And you're bluffing."

"I'm not talking about the Swiss one. I'm talking about *your* secret one."

Jerry paled. "You don't know who you're messing with!"

"No," Zach said, "I think you don't know who *you're* dealing with. Let's recap so I'm sure you have it. Patty is under the protection of Rochester. Don't mess with her. Do you understand?"

The man stared at him, his beady eyes calculating, scheming. He was angry for being cornered, for losing ground in his own game.

"Do you understand?" Zach repeated slowly.

"You really don't know who you're dealing with."

Zach moved to the window, giving it a light tap. On the other side, Logan tapped back. Zach gave a small nod.

"What are you doing?" Jerry asked nervously. "What was that about?"

"I hope you weren't planning to do anything with the funds in your secret-secret bank account." He moved toward the door. "How fast can you get back to the UK?" He turned to consider the sweating man. "Faster than Rochester can find your girlfriend?" When Jerry seethed silently, Zach added casually, "I heard you're a betting man."

"No!" the man yelled.

Zach continued to the door. He gave it a light rap to indicate he was ready to leave.

Jerry let out a string of curses. "I get it! You win. I understand. I understand! Just leave me alone and I'll leave Patty alone."

The latch unlocked with a click and Zach moved through the door, letting it close behind him. There were just a few more loose ends to deal with before he could show Catherine that, with him, she was safe.

15

*C*atherine sat on the bus with Xavier in her lap, fighting tears. Her son was heavy in her arms. The bus lurched out of town, the holiday decorations cheerily brightening the light posts all the way down Main Street.

Zach hadn't tried to stop her. He'd let her walk right out of his life.

He'd said he loved her, then had let her walk away.

Which was good. She couldn't stay, couldn't trust him. She couldn't trust anyone.

But a spy? They were all really spies?

Was that why Zach had a talent with all things security related?

She rubbed her eyes.

He thought he loved her, but he didn't really know her, just like she didn't know him.

She leaned further into her seat. She didn't want to think or feel anymore. She just wanted to get far, far away.

She'd find shelter. Maybe hide in a hotel lobby or hospital waiting room for a few hours, always moving until the night was through. Then find a new town and a new way to become invisible.

How long and how far would she have to go to cover her trail this time?

She had taken Leo's suggestion to marry Zach and come to Blueberry Springs. And she'd been found. What if Jerry had pried the info out of Leo by ruthless means?

It wasn't worth getting close to people. Not when ruthless men like Jerry were still a part of her life.

Not when everyone was full of deception. Leo. Simon. Zach. Even Logan. She was surrounded by agents. But how much was real? How much was a cover?

Had Simon infiltrated her family's dealings with her help?

He hadn't loved her. He'd used her. Then left her.

A tear slipped down her cheek, landing on Xavier's nose, causing him to blink.

She'd let Simon in and he'd used her, put her in danger.

But he had also given her Xavier.

Zach would have been a good father.

But he'd kept things from her.

Just like she'd kept things from him.

Had Simon really planned for her to come here? Was Zach really a retired agent? Or was that all a lie, a cover-up? She shuddered at the memory of how he'd grabbed Jerry and pummeled him without hesitation. He'd said Jerry's name. And he'd defeated the man who always came out on top.

Plus put a target on his own back in the process, most likely.

To keep her safe.

He'd had to fight a killer in his home because of her.

Catherine barely held in the sobs as the bus weaved around the high mountain curves and switchbacks, heading toward the city, where she could lose herself in the crowds, disappear from Zach's life.

A puff of air touched her cheek as someone settled in the bus seat beside her.

Catherine froze, eyes darting that direction.

It was Ginger.

"Hey." The woman looked grim. "I'd been meaning to talk to you about something."

"There's not going to be a reception," Catherine said, trying to rein in her emotions. The pale blue dress she'd ordered would no longer be needed.

"Zach's a retired spy. He used to work with Logan."

"I don't care."

"If I'd have told you, it would have changed things. It takes these guys time to adjust back into civilian life. Zach was sucking at it, and Logan was worried that he'd..." Ginger shook her head of auburn curls. "Zach's changed, you know." Her expression softened. "I tried everything to find the right woman for him and failed. Then you came along." She reached out and touched one of Xavier's perfect little curls. "He loves you. Both of you."

"I'm not coming back. What we had..." Her voice had cracked and she abandoned that line of thought. It was best not to think about it, because it made her feel worse, like she wasn't making the right decision for the right reasons. "It's not safe." She looked at Xavier. It truly wasn't. She had to protect not only herself and her son, but Zach, too. Jerry could have easily gotten the upper hand in that fight earlier. If anything had happened to Zach or Logan it would have been her fault. Jill, too.

And it almost had.

Catherine closed her eyes, trying not to think, not to feel.

"Zach and Logan can help," Ginger said softly.

"My family—people know where I am now. It's not safe for me to stay."

"This is what they do."

"It's my problem." Too many people could get hurt. Good people. If she truly loved Zach, she needed to put space between them.

"They want to help."

Her breath shuddered over the pain in her chest. She loved Zach. Despite all the reasons not to, she did.

"Please come back. Please let them help you," Ginger said.

"You don't know what it's like. Always being on watch, on edge. Wondering. Worrying. I let my guard down. I trusted someone I shouldn't have. I put people at risk."

Even if she could trust Zach, believe he was on the right side, there would always be the fear.

"And it will be better if just you and Xavier are on the run, without anyone at your side to help?"

"Yes," Catherine replied, determined not to think about what it would be like. How exhausting and terrifying it would be now that she'd already been found once.

"Zach's going to worry about you no matter

where you go. He's going to track you, keep an eye on you."

Catherine's heart hurt, thinking about him.

"That'll leave an additional trail," Ginger said. "Even for a fantastic agent. Being retired, he doesn't have access to full agency resources. His shadowing won't be as tight."

"I see what you're doing," Catherine said.

Ginger smiled. "Is it working?"

"No."

She was going to disappear, not just from her life, but from his, too, because that's what you did when you loved someone with all your heart.

ZACH WATCHED Catherine get off the bus in the city of Dakota, a few hours from Blueberry Springs. He'd sped the entire way, passing the bus just before town and letting out a sigh of relief for not losing her. It had been a risk, taking a few minutes back home to deal with Jerry, then tying up a few other loose ends.

She hitched her diaper bag higher on her shoulder and held Xavier protectively. There weren't many people in the bus station, the street-lights casting shadows and making her look vulnerable and alone as she headed inside the building.

She glanced around as though expecting him to be there. To intervene. To stop her.

Or maybe she was making sure nobody familiar was shadowing her, waiting for their moment.

And that was why he was here. He would shadow her for however long it took for him to ensure her safety, while he convinced her to come back into his life.

He watched to see if Ginger got off the bus. She'd climbed on at the last minute back in Blueberry Springs, surprising him with the move. She didn't exit it now.

Through the terminal's long windows Zach saw Catherine enter the ladies' room. He stood outside in the shadows, hunching his coat up over his ears, as he waited for her to come back out.

When she didn't appear right away, he figured she was changing Xavier.

He shifted, making sure he had a good visual of the door and hadn't missed her. Nobody who'd come or gone through it matched her description. Too tall, too short, too skinny, too pregnant. His vantage point was good. There were no other exits. Not even a window to climb out. She had to still be inside.

After about five minutes, he moved away from

his spot. Determined to walk right into the ladies' room to find out what had happened to his wife, he had to sidestep a pregnant woman with short black hair who'd just exited the station.

Something about her tripped a switch in his brain and his steps slowed. He looked over his shoulder, but the woman was moving quickly now. Not waddling in the way he would expect for a woman as far along as she was. And her baby bump was too high. She was hiding something. Or someone.

Xavier.

The woman was Catherine.

CATHERINE FORCED herself not to break into a run. Zach had followed her to the city. He was on her trail.

What was she going to do? Her heart was hammering so hard her chest hurt.

He hadn't recognized her. How could he say he loved her, and then walk right past her without something about her triggering his awareness?

She wanted to take solace in the security of her disguise, but her heart broke with every step she took away from the man she loved. The man she had wanted to raise her son as his own.

She reminded herself to remain vigilant, to keep her eyes up and trained on people, to watch their comings and goings with suspicion. Her time in Blueberry Springs had worn down her constant state of awareness, and she felt the adrenaline kick in as she tried to be ever alert.

She had exited the bus station, and now walked around the building, planning to take a route she'd seen from the bus. She'd walk through the square and into the grand hotel backing onto it. She'd then exit out a side door, heading through whatever mazes she could find, doubling back until she was certain she wasn't being followed.

She froze as she spotted her cousin Jerry standing near the drained fountain in the middle of the wintry square, buildings rising up on either side of him. His hands were deep in his pockets, and he was shifting from foot to foot. There was a lit up Christmas tree behind him, piles of snow along the edges of the cleared footpath, a man standing in the shadows kept an eye trained on Jerry as he smoked a cigarette and laughed with someone. Associates? She glanced left and saw another man waiting along a wall, his face in shadows as he talked into a phone.

How had Jerry escaped? Was Zach okay? Scott? Logan? Who had he hurt to free himself? Who had he harmed to ensure he was here right now? Were those two men his associates? Were there more watching from the shadows? Ready to spring on her if *he* failed to catch her?

She forced herself to keep moving, confident he wouldn't recognize her. As she drew nearer to him, she looked over her shoulder, seeking Zach's comforting large build. He was nowhere to be seen.

She hesitated, feeling alone and vulnerable.

You're in disguise, she reminded herself. *Zach didn't even recognize you.*

She added an extra waddle to her step, and moved past her cousin.

"Excuse me," he said, when she was shoulder to shoulder with him, a mere two feet separating them. She didn't know whether to flee or to stop. "Do you know the time?"

She shook her head, her eyes on the brightly lit entrance to the hotel. There was a doorman there, his head bent as he did something on his phone.

"I was supposed to meet my cousin here," Bucket said. "To tell her that I don't know her."

Confused, Catherine met his eye.

"I don't know her," he said again, his voice shaking. He began backing away and the men she'd seen in the shadows took a step closer. "I don't know her. It's like she never existed. I'll tell everyone she's dead. Tell her that, Patty. Tell her that she just..." He swallowed hard. "That I took care of her. Just tell her that I don't know her!" He was practically shouting now, tripping over himself as he scrambled to get away from her.

Catherine stood by the fountain for a long moment after her cousin had scurried out of sight, the men from the shadows catching up with him in seconds, surrounding him in a cluster as they moved him out of sight.

Behind Catherine slow footsteps approached on the cold bricks.

She turned, ready to fight or flee.

It was Zach. He stopped a few feet away. He had his hands in his coat pockets, and all he said was, "I told you you were safe with me. Now do you believe me?"

16

$\mathcal{C}$atherine was sobbing in Zach's arms. He led her to his car, where it was warm and safe, settling her in the passenger seat. He'd brought Xavier's car seat, she saw, a presumptuous move that made her want to throw herself right back into his arms all over again. But instead of asking to put Xavier, who was sleeping against her chest, into the carrier, he simply gave her a moment to decompress, seemingly not expecting her to come home with him.

Home.

Everything about being with Zach felt like home, and it made her cry harder.

He'd chased off the scariest person she knew.

He was trained to keep people safe, and he had stepped in without being asked and protected her.

He was exactly the kind of person she needed in her life. He was the man she'd been waiting and hoping for, the one she'd given her heart to despite her vow to never trust or let anyone in ever again.

"Was Jerry the cause of the break-ins around town?" She hated to think that she'd not only brought him to Blueberry Springs, but that he may have left the people she cared about fearing their safety.

"No. Scott caught the thieves this morning. They were from a town or two over. Pretty good, but not good enough to avoid getting nabbed."

She sat quietly for a moment.

"And for the record, it wasn't me," Zach said.

"I know," she said quickly, embarrassed to have even considered that it could have been Zach causing the break-ins, and even more so that he'd been able to read her earlier thoughts about it.

"Logan and Scott brought Jerry here to talk to you, to assure you he was no longer going to pursue you. Scott, Logan, and the city officers who helped them as backup still have Jerry in custody. Scott will lay charges on your behalf, but ultimately your cousin will likely be sent back to the UK to continue his sentence. Plus some."

Catherine nodded, relieved that Jerry wasn't on the loose once again, and that he hadn't hurt anyone. "Good."

"I think you should call your father," Zach said.

"What? No. No." She found herself reaching for the door handle.

"Just to confirm where things sit. So you know it's over and nobody's going to come looking for you."

He was holding his cell phone out to her. She looked at it for a long moment. "I don't want him to know where I am."

"Do I look stupid?" Zach asked, his expression so unimpressed that she laughed. "It's a burn phone issued via my old agency. Logan had one on hand." Zach paused, his lips pursing as though he was ticked about something his friend had done. "The signal's untraceable. And anyway, it's not like your dad has caller ID in jail."

Catherine turned the phone over in her hands. "What do I say?"

"What do you think you need to say?"

She wasn't sure. Zach passed her a piece of paper with a phone number and prisoner number written on it. Catherine felt the familiar shame weigh on her as she thought of all her father had done.

"I don't think I can." She had typed in the number, hit the button to connect the call, then clicked off. "And besides, it's too early in the morning over there."

"It's not. And I'm right here with you," Zach said gently. "This is your closure. For you and Xavier. Otherwise you'll always be wondering if someone else is going to come."

This was her chance to have her happily-ever-after and stop running.

She stared out at the dark night for a long moment, trying to rebuild her courage. Instead, she found herself thinking about Zach. He had been fierce and determined today, but gentle and strong, too. She hoped that at the end of this night, she'd feel safe enough to return home with him, to spend the rest of her life at his side.

To have that chance, she needed to make this call.

She hit Redial and this time kept the phone to her ear until someone picked up.

With her heart slamming ruthlessly against her ribs, she gave them her father's prisoner number and waited for several long minutes as he was brought to the phone.

"Daddy?" she said, hating the way her voice sounded so small and trembling. Mixed emotions flooded through her. It didn't matter who he was or what he'd done, he was still her father. He was still the one who had taught her how to ride a bike, how to stand up for herself with pushy boys. He'd been there for her, as misguided as he was corrupt, but in her corner even if he didn't understand her.

"Patty?" His tone was urgent. He sniffed loudly, his voice shaking as much as hers. "Patty, is that really you?"

"It's me."

"Are you safe?" he asked.

The concern in his voice made her throat tighten as she choked out a yes.

He let out a loud, shaky exhalation. "I was so worried. When you disappeared I called in every favor I could, which wasn't easy considering my predicament. Nobody could find you."

"I was hiding."

"I'm so glad you're safe. Do we need to end this call?"

"No. We're okay. I have someone on my side who knows how to take care of business."

"Patty?" There was concern *and* confusion in his voice now and she laughed.

"No, Daddy. He's on the other side." The legal side. But most of all, he was on *her* side. She smiled at Zach, already glad she'd made this call. He deserved a really big kiss for setting this up for her.

"I should have told you to quit that nightclub." He added quickly, panic edging his voice, "Bucket lost his mind while he was in here. He broke out and he's coming for you. He's convinced you're alive, and that you put him in here. He thinks you were behind all of this, but I know you're not. Everyone knows you aren't. I made it clear you were to be kept clean of all of this, but he's not listening to reason."

"Bucket won't bother me, Daddy."

Her father's sharp intake of breath made her laugh. "I didn't ice him."

"You're the one thing I've done right in this life, aren't you?"

Tears streamed down Catherine's face and she said with a wobbly voice, "Pretty much."

They both laughed.

"Everyone who's in here knows it wasn't you, Patty." Her father's tone told her he was winding up the call. "If you're ever in the area, feel free to stop in." He added quickly, "That's not fair. Don't feel like you have to come visit."

"I'll keep it in mind," she said, before ending the call. She hadn't told him he was a grandfather, but she figured that could be for another day. Today, this was enough.

She turned to Zach. "Take me home."

17

*Z*ach stood at the front of the church, waiting for Catherine to come down the aisle.

They were having a wedding. One that would fulfill Catherine's dream, and would ensure the legality of their online union, too.

A wedding even though he still hadn't proposed. When the ladies had begun finalizing the reception plans for the wine and cheese, Zach had taken Catherine over to Ginger's shop and told her to pick out a gown.

She'd frowned at him and he'd leaned over, whispering, "Let's have a wedding before the reception. Small, private. Get that little tuxedo for Xavier. Get the dress. We'll beg Olivia to put a rush on it. Let's do this right."

She'd tipped away from him so she could take in the sincerity of his suggestion. Then a slow, wide smile had graced her beautiful face and she'd thrown herself into his arms with a laugh.

He'd held her, knowing that they were merely at the beginning of something truly magical.

He adjusted his bow tie now and waited for Catherine to appear. Ginger, one of the two bridesmaids, was in the doorway, waiting for her cue to come down the aisle. She grinned at Zach and flashed him a thumbs-up.

Xavier was already halfway down the aisle, handsome in his stroller, a string of drool threatening to mar his perfect tux as one of the flower girls pushed him and the ring cushion toward the front of the church.

Family.

Real life.

He'd done it. He glanced at Logan, who was behind him, standing as best man.

Logan gave him a lift of his chin in silent support.

"Thanks for having my back," Zach said.

His friend nodded, before his gaze drifted toward his wife, who was coming down the aisle in a gorgeous red satin dress that hugged her curves. Ginger was followed by Jill, but the bridesmaids weren't what Zach was focused on, knowing that

Catherine would soon be coming through that doorway.

After what felt like forever, the music changed, and a woman in a white dress appeared, her smile brightening the entire room as she came toward him, her blue eyes locked on his.

His wife. His partner. His friend. His soulmate.

He found himself coming down the aisle to meet her halfway. She had a long veil that trailed down her back, but the piece covering her face was short and soft, and he flipped it up, kissing her right there in the middle of the church. Their few guests laughed and cheered at his break in protocol.

Zach never wanted to stop kissing his wife, but when he forced himself to break the connection, she smiled, her eyes glittering, her heart completely open. "You're such a rule breaker."

"Speaking of which, I need to ask you something."

"I'm busy right now. Can I just say yes and renege later if need be?"

He dropped to one knee. "Catherine, will you marry me?"

She gave him a dry look and stuck out one hip, the light catching on the beaded design along her bodice, enhancing her curves.

He held up the engagement ring he'd been carrying around for weeks, assuming he'd find a chance before now to give it to her. Her mouth dropped open and he saw in her expression that he'd done the right thing.

"We really have issues with doing all of this in order, don't we?" she said, and held out her trembling left hand.

He clasped it and repeated, "Will you marry me?"

"Only if we have the wedding immediately."

He grinned and slid the ring on her finger. "Is that a yes?"

"It's a yes."

She slipped her hand in his, and they walked to the front of the church, ready to be married, legally bound in ways that their hearts and souls already were.

CATHERINE STOOD beside Zach in Brew Babies, which had been decorated to the hilt, looking festive and beautiful with streamers and balloons. Classy. She smiled for a photo, no longer worried that it would be uploaded to social media, and that someone would use facial recognition to track her.

She was free.

Freer than she had ever been in her whole entire life, and it felt good. It felt as though she could fly, swooping above the mountain peaks that surrounded the tiny town.

She was home.

She was family.

She was love.

She had a man who knew exactly who she was and loved her just the same.

Turning to Zach, she said, "I love you."

"You keep saying that."

"Because it's true."

"Okay, so wait a second," Ginger said, coming over, hands out like she needed to brace herself. "You didn't actually order Catherine online?" She was giving him a hopeful look, as if his very image depended upon the answer.

Catherine and Zach exchanged a glance. Their story was getting out, and as in most small towns, the gossip, rumors and truth were all mixed up.

"I did but I didn't," Zach said.

Logan joined them, slipping an arm around his wife's shoulders. "MI6 may have had a helping hand in setting up these two."

Catherine had been shocked when she'd learned the truth. Both that Zach hadn't fessed up to her about not recalling their live chats from back when they'd begun "dating" online, as well as the fact that an agent had been masquerading as him, sending messages on his behalf and essentially manipulating situations so she'd feel as though escaping to Blueberry Springs and marrying Zach was her safest bet. The whole time she'd been on the run she'd thought she'd dodged danger and was successful in hiding, but the entire time she'd been watched. Yet it had brought her here. Brought her to the life she'd always dreamed of having.

"I guess they're just better at matchmaking," Logan said, trying to withhold a smile as he teased his wife.

She socked him gently in the shoulder and said, "Not funny!"

"Come buy me a beer," Logan said, extracting himself and Zach from the women.

"Chickens!" Ginger called after them. They turned around at the same time, both flashing massive smiles.

"Run away!" Catherine teased.

"It's what Team Pancake does," Zach retorted.

"I think you just might be a member of Team Waffle, Mr. Forrester," she called after him. "You're mighty complex."

He sent her a private smile that warmed her insides just before Logan pulled him into a group of men standing at the bar.

Jill passed by with Xavier, dancing to a Frank Sinatra tune coming from the jukebox. Catherine laughed and held out her arms for her boy, who gave her a grin.

"There's your baby," Jill said, transferring him into Catherine's arms. "I told Burke that my womb is twitching."

"And?" Ginger asked.

The woman smiled. "He told me we should start trying, because you never know what tomorrow will bring."

Catherine and she exchanged smiles, still unable to talk about the fearful moment with Jerry where everything could have gone terribly wrong.

Ginger was squealing at the baby news, and Catherine said, "Let me know when you need baby clothes."

The crush of people who'd come out to celebrate with them parted for a moment, and Catherine spied Cole sitting alone at the bar with his usual three o'clock shot of whiskey.

"Has anyone figured out what he's contemplating every afternoon?" she asked.

Jill shrugged. "He came to climb some mountains a few years ago and forgot to go home. He's probably trying to decide when he should return to Texas."

Catherine raised a brow at Ginger. "He's been in town for how many years and he's *still* single?"

"He wasn't looking," Ginger said with a huff. "Because trust me, I tried."

"Oh, I bet he has someone back home who left his heart in tatters." Jill was grinning, enjoying Ginger's lack of success with the cowboy.

The pub went silent as the main doors swung open, letting a shaft of December sunshine into the room. A cowboy was standing in the doorway, his stance wide, like he'd just got off a horse. He tipped his hat to Mary Alice and Liz.

"I'm looking for my brother, Cole Wylder."

The whole pub hushed as all eyes swung to Cole. He didn't respond right away, just lowered his head. Then his chest and back expanded as he inhaled and spun on his stool, turning to face the man with the same summer sky-blue eyes.

"What do you want, Brant?"

The stranger remained in the doorway, his frame swaying slightly as if he wanted to embrace his long-lost brother, but the code of cowboy stoicism prevented him from making any kind of gesture or scene.

"I'm not airing our family business here, but if you ever plan on returning home, now's the time." And with that, Cole's brother tipped his hat, pivoted on the heel of one cowboy boot and headed through the still-open door, letting it shut silently behind him.

Ginger turned to Catherine, eyes wide with excitement.

"Now Brant? He's single. And he's looking. Far and wide."

"For his brother," Catherine said with a half giggle.

"No," Ginger said quietly, her eyes narrowed in thought. "He's looking for his Mrs. Right, and he's going to find her. And so is Cole. I promise."

VEILS AND VOWS

Find love in unexpected places with these sweet marriage of convenience romances.

The Promise (Book 0: Devon & Olivia)

The Surprise Wedding (Book 1: Devon & Olivia)

A Pinch of Commitment (Book 2: Ethan & Lily)

The Wedding Plan (Book 3: Luke & Emma)

Accidentally Married (Book 4: Burke & Jill)

The Marriage Pledge (Book 5: Moe & Amy)

Mail Order Soulmate (Book 6: Zach & Catherine)

ALSO BY JEAN ORAM

FREE EBOOK

Blueberry Springs

Read, Dream, Laugh & Love
Sweet, Laugh-out-Loud Romances

Have you fallen in love with Blueberry Springs? Catch up with your friends and their adventures...

Book 1: Whiskey and Gumdrops (Mandy & Frankie)

Book 2: Rum and Raindrops (Jen & Rob)

Book 3: Eggnog and Candy Canes (Katie & Nash)

Book 4: Sweet Treats (3 short stories—Mandy, Amber, & Nicola)

Book 5: Vodka and Chocolate Drops (Amber & Scott)

Book 6: Tequila and Candy Drops (Nicola & Todd)

Companion Novel: Champagne and Lemon Drops (Beth & Oz)

THE SUMMER SISTERS

Taming billionaires has never been so *sweet*.

Falling for billionaires has never been so sweet.

* Available in paperback & ebook & audio! *

One cottage. Four sisters. And four billionaires who will sweep them off their feet.

Falling for the Movie Star

Falling for the Boss

Falling for the Single Dad

Falling for the Bodyguard

Falling for the Firefighter

ABOUT THE AUTHOR

 Jean Oram is a *New York Times* and *USA Today* best-selling romance author. Inspiration for her small town series came from her own upbringing on the Canadian prairies. Although, so far, none of her characters have grown up in an old schoolhouse or worked on a bee farm. Jean still lives on the prairie with her husband, two kids, and big shaggy dog where she can be found out playing in the snow or hiking.

Become an Official Fan:
www.facebook.com/groups/jeanoramfans
Newsletter: www.jeanoram.com/FREEBOOK
Twitter: www.twitter.com/jeanoram
Instagram: www.instagram.com/author_jeanoram
Facebook: www.facebook.com/JeanOramAuthor
Website & blog: www.jeanoram.com

Made in United States
North Haven, CT
26 March 2023

34581467R00209